Praise for Christopher Meeks's First Short Story Collection, *The Middle-Aged Man and the Sea*:

"A collection that is so stunning...that I could not help but move on to the next story."
— ***Entertainment Weekly***

"Poignant and wise, sympathetic to the everyday struggles these characters face."
— ***Los Angeles Times***

"These are original, articulate, engaging stories which examine life in America from the unique perspectives of ordinary people searching for their share of the promises held out as part of the American dream.... *The Middle-Aged Man and The Sea* is highly recommended, highly entertaining, highly rewarding reading."
— ***The Midwest Book Review***

"Christopher Meeks bounces onto the literary scene as a vibrant new voice filled with talent and imagination. *The Middle-Aged Man and the Sea* is one of the finer collections of short stories that will rapidly rise to the top to of the heap of a battery of fine writers of this difficult medium."
— **Grady Harp, Top Ten Reviewer,**
   Amazon.com

"Mr. Meeks has a wonderfully fun writing style—witty, cynical, and often poignant. His stories are about the stuff of life: love and heartbreak, sickness and death, desires and struggles, spirituality and the search for meaning."
— **Janet Rubin, *Novel Reviews***

"In this collection of short stories, Christopher Meeks examines the small heartbreaks and quiet despair that are so much a part of all of our lives. He does it in language that is resonant, poetic, and precise. Franz Kafka said that a book should be an ice-axe to break the frozen sea within us. This collection is just such a weapon. If you like Raymond Carver, you'll love Meeks. He may be as good—or better. He deserves major recognition."
— **author David Scott Milton** (*Paradise Road*)

Acclaim for Christopher Meeks's Second Story Collection, *Months and Seasons*:

"The stories in *Months and Seasons* are like potato chips: you can't read just one. Just a few sentences into the first piece, "Dracula Slinks into the Night," I immediately felt at home in the world Meeks has created."
— **Marc Schuster, *Small Press Reviews***

"For those readers fortunate enough to have read Christopher Meeks's first short story collection, *The Middle-Aged Man and the Sea,* and discovered the idiosyncrasies of Meeks's writing style and content, rest assured that this new collection, *Months and Seasons,* not only will not disappoint, but also it will provide further proof that we have a superior writer of the genre in our presence."
— **Grady Harp, Top Ten Reviewer, Amazon.com**

"With this collection, Christopher Meeks proves there is an audience for short stories. His characters are well defined with problems that they can't resolve. There are twelve tales that reveal a lot about our present society. Meeks's stories reminded me of those of John Cheever."
— **Gary Roen,** *The Midwest Book Review*

"Full of complete randomness and quirkiness, ingredients I cherish, the stories in this twelve-story collection chronicle the eccentricities of an array of diverse characters, who are dealing with life thrown at them in the only way actually possible: by dealing with their problems, not escaping them."
— **Rachel Durfor,** *Rebecca's Reads*

"I am pleased to report that if *Months and Seasons*, the new collection from Christopher Meeks, was a music album, many of its twelve pieces would be destined for the charts – no filler here."
— **Sam Sattler,** *Book Chase*

"*Months and Seasons* is very different from the recent collections I reviewed by Jhumpa Lahiri and Sana Krasikov. His characters are quirky and unpredictable and the stories are refreshingly modern. From Halloween parties in L.A. to a summer camp in northern Minnesota, his characters never seem to do the expected thing."
— **Lisa Hura,** *Minds Alive on the Shelves*

"Meeks's talent at exploring the power dynamics within relationships, almost exclusively between men and women, is fascinating."
— **Rebecca Swaney,** *Adventures in Reading*

Novels by Christopher Meeks

The Brightest Moon of the Century

Love at Absolute Zero

Blood Drama

A Death in Vegas

The Chords of War

Other Short Story Collections

The Middle-Aged Man and the Sea

Months and Seasons

Play

Who Lives?

The Benefits of Breathing

For Deborah —
Enjoy!
Christopher Meeks

Stories by Christopher Meeks
Foreword by Roderick Clark

White Whisker Books
Los Angeles

ISBN 978-0-9863265-5-4
Library of Congress Control Number:
Copyright © 2020 by Christopher Meeks
First Edition

Library of Congress Cataloging-in-Publication Data

Meeks, Christopher.
    The benefits of breathing / by Christopher Meeks — 1st ed.
        p. cm.
1. United States – Social life and customs – 21st century—Fiction.
PS3613.E374 B46 2020
813.6

Editor, Carol Fuchs

Cover Design: OliviaProDesign at Fiverr.com

White Whisker Books, Los Angeles

Dedicated to Cynthia Klar and her daughter, Nicki

Contents

"You Wreck Me, Baby" first appeared in *Rosebud,* Issue 60

"Jerry with a Twist" first appeared in *Rosebud,* Issue 63

"Incident on South Cecilia" first appeared in *Lit Noir,* Issue 11, and then
    reprinted in *Rosebud,* Issue 56

"A Warm Front Appears to be Moving from California and Deep into Minnesota"
    first appeared in a different version in *Rosebud,* Issue 59

"I'd Rather Die than Go to North Dakota" first appeared in *Lit Noir,* Issue 4

The rest of the stories first appeared as Amazon Shorts.

Foreword

It's all about love, isn't it? Under all the emotional geology, under all the subtle narrative layers of Christopher Meeks's stories, love is lurking. Love sought, love missing, love wrought with difficulty: love tangled and unfathomable, love lost and found.

Not that there isn't plenty of the rest of life written about in these tales—engaging life, approaching death, the struggles with economics, entropy, and expectations: the pursuit of perfect happiness that always seems just out of reach. But love is like water. While water may not be on our minds at every moment of our existence, we know we can't possibly live without it, or at the very least the hope that we can find it, clarify it, hold on to it for dear life....

There's another current, too, in these stories, the sense that everything we feel is mixed with everything else, the weather, the sunlight on our skin, encircling places and people, a fly on the wall, the scent of the grass.

The contexts are perpetually modern, carrying the reader forward in a streaming "nowness." The protagonists are a lot like our quotidian selves, generally middle class, but not without financial anxiety

– resilient in coping, but with vulnerability always front and center. Here are the pushes and pulls we all experience: head tangling with heart as in his novel, *Love at Absolute Zero*; rootedness vs. dislocation, as in "I'd Rather Die than Move to North Dakota;" separation vs. staying together, as in "You Wreck me, Baby."

In whatever territory he covers, Meeks is surefooted. We have been there. We have seen these people. And in a sense, we *become* them as we read.

With this collection we see a truly American voice emerging from a suburban landscape, inching toward greatness, turf that Meeks will undoubtedly inherit.

--Roderick Clark, Editor/Publisher
Rosebud Magazine

Joni Paredes

The steel doors of the hotel elevator opened with a whisper, like the wind rushing through the cracks of a marble mausoleum. With her dark shoulder-length hair bouncing, Joni Paredes stepped out and strode down the hotel's elegant hallway as if she owned the place. Put on a smile, put on a smile, she told herself. Athena would be a beautiful bride but was probably going nuts. Joni knocked at the right door.

"Mom?" came the voice, higher than usual.

"It's the Easter Bunny." Too ironic? Joni added the word "Honey."

The door swung open, and her daughter, Athena, gorgeous, thin, and far too young, charged at her in a flash of white and hugged her. Joni wasn't a huggy person generally, but for her daughter, anything.

"I didn't think I'd be so nervous today," Athena said.

Joni smiled as they hugged. Her daughter just didn't know herself.

Joni glimpsed at the room that Athena and Glen would share that night. The king-sized bed was angled toward a view of palm treetops and greener Pasadena. Fresh red roses stood in a clear vase on an antique writing desk. A painting of a bowl of fruit hung on the wall by the heavy blue-and-gold window side panels. The money Joni was spending was worth it.

Athena pulled back and gazed, now aghast, at her mother. "You're wearing that dress today?"

Joni frowned. "What's wrong? It's a nice dress—a dress worthy of my only child."

"It's red! As usual, are you trying to take away my spotlight?"

"As usual? What?"

"Red?"

"It has flowers on it," Joni said.

"Bold Georgia O'Keefe flowers."

"It's okay. You're just nervous." Joni straightened the shoulders on the gown. "You probably want to get out of this—don't want to wrinkle it yet. Then let me take you to breakfast."

"Can I be in charge for once? It's my day."

"What do you want to do?"

"Go to breakfast, not in this dress."

Joni threw her hands in the air and said, "Are you listening, God?"

"Don't be that way," said Athena. "At least give me the illusion I have choice."

"You're marrying, aren't you? That's your choice."

Athena started pulling off her gown, and Joni stepped behind her to help.

"You said you loved Glen," said Athena.

"Of course I do," said Joni.

"You accept him, I think. Love? That'd be a stretch."

"Now you're telling me how I feel? I'm very fond of him."

"Yeah. That's what I thought," Athena said, sounding disappointed.

A feeling, an odd rumble, hit Joni in the pit of her stomach, something she hadn't felt since she slept under a staircase at sixteen, having run away from home. Panic.

She pushed at that feeling, demanding it leave. "Athena, come on. Let's have breakfast."

"I'm not going to be like you," said Athena. "Glen and I are for keeps."

"Really?" Joni wanted to spank her—something Joni hadn't done since Athena was two, when she wouldn't stop crying about a French fry that had dropped on the ground.

Athena pulled the last of her gown off and tossed it hard on the bed. "This is exactly why we have to talk. On my twenty-first birthday three weeks ago, we got those damn wolf-head tattoos on our butts to match each other. What was that, a cattle brand for me?"

"You thought it was a cute idea!"

"I know you wanted it—ten whiskers on my wolf's face, eleven on yours, to make twenty-one. Cute. I did it to prove you aren't losing me."

"What? Just because you were a psychology major doesn't make you Freud."

"You love 'em and leave 'em," said Athena. "You never even take their phone calls or texts after you decide it's over."

"My dates?"

"Yeah. Your Match.com guys. You're like a presidential game-show host: 'You're fired.'"

"Just a couple cases, and they weren't my type." The image of her late husband on the bed with all that blood flashed in her mind. "Can we *not* talk about this? Don't ruin your day."

Joni had dated a yoga teacher once for three dates. She couldn't stand his analyzing what she ate. "All that meat," he'd said, as if it were some strange psychosis, especially the pork. Still earlier, he had explained his breathing technique in beginning yoga. First breathe so air fills the lower belly, then fill the lower rib cage, and move up into the throat and nose. He'd called it "ocean breathing," which sounded like bullshit at the time, but then when she was alone in bed, inhaling and exhaling through her nose, it did have an ocean sound. She found it helped her control any flare of anger, especially as she focused on the air in her nose. Now, as Joni made herself busy by hanging the dress in the closet, she breathed, starting at her belly and moving up to her nose.

Once calm, she said, "Is this Slam Mom Day? If you want me to change my dress, I'll go home. I have plenty of others. Blue? Is that acceptable?"

"Can't you listen to me for once?"

Joni turned sharply. "What has gotten into you? You don't want to marry Glen?"

"Of course I do!" Athena said, poking the air for punctuation. "You think you're losing me, right? You're not. But Glen and I are going to move to another state."

"What? Where? I can't just up and leave."

"Seattle. And you're not invited. Glen got a job there. I'm going to get a graduate degree in psychology at the U of W. I'm good at psych. That's how I can see into you."

Joni waved it off, then straightened her collar in the mirror.

"You made sure, when I was a tween," said Athena, "that I knew about birth control. You sent me to the best schools. You've been a good mom, yet the way you run your life with men, you don't think I notice?"

"I'm just picky. I can be picky, can't I?"

"That's what you call it."

"What do you have against me today?" said Joni. "I do everything for you."

"Are you going to give me the speech about birthing me at seventeen? My cocaine-addled father?"

"Honey, honey, calm down. It's your wedding day."

"I know you think I'm too young."

"We're not going to get into this today. Today is for fun."

"*You* married at twenty-one," Athena said.

"And how well did that work out?"

"So you're 'fond' of Glen."

"Listen, I'm going to meet you in the Terrace dining room in a few minutes, okay?" With that, Joni left.

Back in the hallway, Joni found herself shaking. Breathe, she told herself. Breathe fucking deep. Only Athena could do this to her, and Joni didn't like being this way. Joni was a person who could control her feelings, and, frankly, she needed to keep doing that.

Glen, a thin young man, had recently landed his first job out of college in Los Angeles as an insurance actuary. He helped calculate risk assessment and figure out insurance premiums. He stood on the lawn with Athena under the wedding arbor. Was he going to work for his same company in Seattle? He'd been a math major at UCLA— what calculations had he done in getting into Athena's heart? As Joni stared at Glen in his tuxedo next to Athena, the sun revealed a red hue in his closely cropped hair.

Who dates a math major, especially one so skinny? Joni wondered. She sat in the front row of the ceremony, which had just started—on a white chair on the green perfect grass of the grand hotel. Why had Athena been attracted to him? Was it because Glen was a type that Joni wouldn't have selected? In the last four months on Match.com, Joni had seen two men, an airplane pilot and a columnist from the business section of the *Los Angeles Times*. Both had been nice, but they started falling in love with her too fast. They'd probably be too emotional, like her late husband. She didn't need that. They didn't get beyond a handful of nice dinners, a concert in one case and a flea market in the other – plus a few evenings of sex, which hit the spot each time.

Didn't Athena understand that she, Joni, left men the way she did because it was clean? Joni was dignified and emailed them. They'd realize she was not their soulmate. Once Joni could see the futures they projected on her, and that was not what she wanted, she left. She was a doer, and she had most everything she needed in life: a good car, no debt, and a great kid. Joni was still young, thirty-eight, so no need to rush into anything.

As Joni watched Glen put the ring on Athena's finger, she thought of his pure devotion. Joni liked that about him and wondered what she would do if she found such a match. Either of those two men she'd recently dated could have become devoted, but it was a man's world, and she didn't need a man telling her what to do. If she could only find the right guy who wasn't that way.

The wedding continued without a hitch with Reverend Jim from the Church of Good Luck officiating. The man was a friend's father, someone, as Athena explained, who had a great sense of humor and loved collecting old-fashioned pinball machines. When Joni had met the reverend, she asked him why one needs a whole church for good luck. He said, "It's to increase one's good fortune and protect the luck you have. Have you had good luck?"

"Do you call having a bitch of a mother whose boyfriend burned my hand over an open flame when I was seven bad luck? Or my running away and getting pregnant at sixteen bad luck?"

"So you'd been victimized," Reverend Jim said.

"No. I'm in control of my life, not luck."

"We're talking the same thing," he said with a smile. "I like you."

From that instant, she liked him.

Now Joni was at the head table in the Georgian Ballroom across from Reverend Jim and next to one of Glen's uncles, a man who was a professor of filmic something at USC's School of Cinema. She guessed he was ten years older than she, and he was half a head taller, with wonderfully dark thick hair and a charming smile. He mentioned he was divorced.

Did Athena place him here purposely? Joni glanced at Athena, who chatted with her bridesmaid, Monica, the girlfriend with great white teeth. As if feeling the stare, Athena glanced over at her mother and smiled. Joni smirked, shook her head at her daughter, and turned back to this Stewart something-or-other.

"Have you ever seen anything by Stanley Kubrick?" Stewart asked. "Such as *2001: A Space Odyssey* or *Full Metal Jacket?*

"I don't go to movies very often," Joni said.

He looked down as if he'd sat at the wrong table.

"I don't mean to be negative," she said, "but movies just seem a great way to use up time and money."

He shook his head and said, "Someone must have treated you wrong."

"Why would you say that?" said Joni.

"Movies are just stories," he said, "but stories help us live. Until the printing press, most stories were passed down orally, but they were vital to people. The Vikings told the Icelandic tales through the dark winter. The Greeks passed along Helen of Troy."

She held up one finger to interrupt. "And everyone talks about *Game of Thrones* now, as if it were a real thing. I'm sorry, but it's just made up, all to eat up our time."

He smiled broadly, wildly shaking his head. "You're missing out. The Bible stories are just metaphors, otherwise made-up, so—"

"Watch it," she said with a laugh. "I'm Catholic."

"Most of the Bible didn't really happen, but it's illustrative. The Greek myths didn't really happen but they absolutely show how people are. Same with all of Shakespeare—same with even *Spiderman* movies and *The Dark*

Knight. The point is we need stories to live, and movies and TV, the best of them, help us."

"That's a lot of power you're putting into movies," Joni said.

"It's no different from your dreams. Your dreams are your brain working out problems, and while most people don't analyze what it means, dreams work on a subconscious level. Same with movies."

"I did see *2001* at the Cinerama Dome. Incredibly weird. I liked how the guy overcame HAL the computer. I remember HAL. I didn't get the ending. I didn't get the metaphor."

"Few people do – but think of Odysseus returning home," said Stewart.

"Okay," she said, not knowing who Odysseus was.

"It's the journey's end, is all. Like the end of *The Wizard of Oz,* there's no place like home."

She laughed and said, "Oil can, oil can," with clenched teeth like the Tin Woodsman. "Okay. Maybe I'll see more movies." She liked the guy.

He smiled again and looked right in her eyes. "I'm sorry. Are you Athena's sister? I missed the connection."

"I'm her mother."

He looked astounded. "You look so young."

"I had her young."

Glancing at her nametag in front of her place setting, he said, "Is there a Mr. Paredes?"

"You don't dither around, do you? Mr. Paredes died four years ago," she said.

"A widow then."

That stopped her for a second. "I guess so. I never think of myself that way—seems for older women. But, yeah, he died young—a nice guy otherwise."

"Sorry for your loss."

She nodded, looking appropriately subdued, even if she thought of her dear hubby as a chickenshit for shooting himself in the head after she left him. She had left saying she loved him, but he had to stop drinking. It had been his big weakness. His gun turned out to be one way to stop.

Joni noticed Stewart staring at her bracelet, a yellow gold Bismark-link bracelet with a lobster clasp that she had found at Macy's once. Matias had noticed her looking at it and then he'd given it to her on a Valentine's Day. It was one of only two things she still had from him. Everything else, she had thrown out.

"That's a beautiful bracelet," he said.

"My daughter gave it to me," she said and looked over at Athena. Stewart looked, too.

"Nice daughter," he said.

"The best."

Again he looked in her eyes, as if trying to look into her soul. She couldn't remember the last time someone did this.

"I'm glad Glen put me here," he said. "What do you do for a living?"

"Gosh, I feel I'm on Match.com."

"I didn't mean—"

"Kidding. I have my own real estate and property management company. I specialize in selling apartment buildings as well as managing some buildings for owners. I have a staff of twelve."

"You're self-made then?"

"Yes—from single teenage mother to computer programmer to being my own boss. I love it."

"Impressive."

"Thank you."

"Plus you have a great smile and voice."

Who was this guy? He made her smile.

After dinner, a live band took to the stage and the singer, a woman with an Irish accent, said, "We're the band The Blesséd Union—great name for a wedding band, right? And we have a first song request from the bride, Pink Floyd's 'Wish You Were Here,' in memory of her father."

"Stepfather, actually," she told Stewart. "But they were close."

"I love Pink Floyd," he said.

"Did my daughter tell you to say that?"

"No, why?"

"I love the band, too."

The band leader said, "We learned this song for tonight, took out the long guitar solos, and we have a beautiful version. It's danceable."

"Want to dance?" she asked Stewart.

He looked surprised and said, "I was getting up the nerve to ask you."

"You don't need to be nervous around me."

"I'm not so sure about that—and I'd love to dance."

They started apart, but the song was tender, written about a missing band member, yet the words could fit many people, talking about fears and years and souls and bowls, and it was so loving and smooth, and Joni and Stewart found a groove. They came together and held each other at the waists, smiling whenever their eyes met. It was nothing she could explain. She hadn't planned on meeting anyone at the wedding. The only plan she had had was to make sure the wedding planners were doing their job. Now Joni didn't even think of them. She did what she did rarely, just let herself go and see where the tide of time took her.

When Joni caught Athena smiling at her as Athena danced with Glen, Joni smiled back. All was forgiven.

At the end of the night, after the dancing, the toasts at the cake cutting, the flower toss, and the good-byes to the hundred guests, Stewart said, "Joni, thank you for the pleasant evening."

"Do you think we could meet again?" she asked.

"Like a Match.com date, you mean?"

She nodded. "No online emailing necessary. Let's just go have fun. What do you like to do for fun?"

"Do you bowl?"

"I'm terrible at it," she said.

"Me, too. Let's do it!"

She pulled out a pen from her small clutch purse—she wasn't a big-purse woman—and she wrote down her phone number and home address on the back of her business card for Pine Crest Realty.

"Here," she said. "Give me a call, and we'll set up a time and place. Want me to research where a bowling alley is?"

"Now that I have your address, I'll find the closest one."

Days later, they sucked at bowling, but scoring was done automatically now by computer, and they clapped for each other when they knocked down pins. They even made one strike each, drank a lot of beer, and slid pizza down their throats.

Over the next few weeks, they saw each other often. She took him walking in the hills above the Descanso Gardens before and just after sunset, and they witnessed the lights of the city come on. The tall distant buildings of Los Angeles looked like a movie set, all sparkle and golden light.

While walking, she asked how long he'd been divorced. Three years. He and his wife Miranda had been married fifteen years, and she'd had an affair. Normally, this information would have been a red flag for Joni, as it meant he could have trust issues. Still, he said only nice things about her, that she'd been very introverted and never told him how lonely she started feeling in marriage. "I'd sensed something going on with Miranda," he'd said, "but she said she was fine." He said they had an amicable divorce, and he was able to buy a house in Pasadena for himself afterwards.

The next weekend, Stewart took Joni to the planetarium at Griffith Park. She'd never been to one before—she'd never thought of it. The stars were so beautiful and the solar system so endless. How could there be no end? At the end of the universe, what was on the other side? As they walked out of the planetarium, he asked, "So? What did you think?"

"The stars are so amazingly beautiful, like beach sand glowing. It's too bad in Los Angeles we can only see a handful of stars at night. It must be amazing to live in, like, Bumfuck Idaho."

He laughed. "Can't say I've been to that town."

"But it did freak me out that there were a billion stars in our galaxy alone—and a billion more galaxies. How is that possible?"

"Less than a hundred years ago, we thought there was only one galaxy, the Milky Way, and that we were in the center of it."

"We're in the center of nothing. We're just little lost souls swimming in a fishbowl, year after year."

"A Floyd song!"

"Until we don't swim anymore? Then what? Even our ashes would be nothing compared to the vastness of the universe. Do we need one more apartment building in it?"

"In L.A., we do," he said.

As they walked to the car from the Griffith Observatory, Stewart took her hand, gently swung her around, and they kissed, slowly at first, as they'd done a few times when he dropped her off at her home, but this time, they stayed at it. This felt so much better than being lost in space. She nibbled at his lips, and he responded in kind. She pushed her tongue into his mouth, and then he did the same thing. They hugged each other with emphasis. She looked down the canyon into Griffith Park, trees, road and—was that the flash of a deer? Everything seemed so perfect.

She said, "Should I come to your house? A sex date?"

He smiled. "I've never heard that term before, but I have to tell you something about me. My marriage counselor said I bond perhaps too easily, so I want to hold off sleeping with you just now."

"Really?" No one had ever turned her down before.

"Believe me, I could eat you up right now," he said. "I'm extremely attracted. I sense we have something special, so I don't want to rush into things with you. I want to do this right."

"Oh," she said. This surprised her. Her first instinct was to say forget it, you're fired, but... this man was different. Most guys would have stripped naked on a first date with her, if given the opportunity. This, strangely, made her more curious about him.

"I'm an INTJ," she said.

"Pardon me? Is that something to do with astrology?"

"No. Athena was a psychology major, and she gave me this test, Myers-Briggs. I came out as an INTJ."

"Oh. Oh, that. When Miranda and I were in marriage counseling, the counselor gave us that test. I was an EN something, but I don't remember what it all means."

"My 'I' is for introvert and you're an 'E,' extrovert."

"Introvert? You don't seem like that. You like to take charge."

"That's what INTJ's do. You're an extrovert, so we probably match well. I'm saying I will wait for when you're ready."

She'd gone out with a few rich guys before, and they had wined and dined her at expensive restaurants. They'd had a sense of entitlement as they tried to seduce her. Once she felt that she had to "give it up" as if it were a payment for a fancy dinner, that's where those dates stopped. Stewart seemed truly interested in her, and the fact he didn't want sex now, well, that made him unique.

They kissed again, and he was great. She knew he'd come around.

During the week, she worked hard with two new clients. She found time to email back and forth with Stewart, and she talked with him once on the phone. On that Friday, she had lunch with Kim, her company's legal advisor. Kim wrote the contracts for all the negotiating Joni did. When they lunched together, they usually finished business quickly and then tried to figure out how men worked, their endless quest.

Kim, a short brunette who men might describe as voluptuous, was on her third husband. Joni told her how Stewart had turned down sex.

"Is he gay?" Kim asked.

"Definitely not. He's an incredible kisser—maybe the best ever. Guys usually kiss impatiently, in hopes to get to the magic box," said Joni, now laughing. "This guy—I feel he's trying to find my soul."

"Do you have one?" she said, smiling.

"Kim!"

"Of course, you have one," she said, looking suddenly contrite. "It's just, well, you run things, right?"

"What's that mean?"

"I mean... I'm sorry." Kim looked worried. Joni thought who was Kim to talk to her boss that way? Joni let her stumble on. "As we've talked about," said Kim. "If a woman takes charge in anything, some men feel threatened."

Joni nodded. "I see. You're right. I thought you meant— never mind. I have a soul like everyone, like you. I don't think Stewart is threatened in the least."

"That's good," said Kim, quickly drinking her water. "Love at first sight, eh?'

"Love is an overused word," said Joni. "Stewart is more than lust, though. Kind of scares me." Joni realized she didn't mean to say that, so added, "in a sexy way, of course."

"Of course. Good luck, lady. Sounds like a keeper."

As they walked back to the office, a gold Toyota Camry passed them, exactly like her last car. It was a great car while she had it. She hadn't kept it long.

Before Joni saw Stewart next, she and Athena met in Koreatown for their monthly scrub and massage. Joni hadn't seen Athena in weeks as Athena had just returned from her honeymoon in Maui—Joni's wedding gift to them besides the wedding.

Joni always felt so clean after Koreatown. An entire body scrub always felt great, like an immaculate house, even if the freshness didn't last. The woman she used, Somi, would press hard, even around and on her breasts, artificially firm due to implants after a breast cancer scare at age thirty. Joni had had a double mastectomy, leaving her chest with loose skin until reconstruction. Matias had been so supportive. "You are everything to me," he'd said. "You're alive! I so love you!"

Then two years later, Joni had reconstruction by a master. There were two downsides, though. She wanted what she had had, a C-cup size. When she went to buy her first new bra at Victoria's Secret, the woman who fitted her insisted she was a D. "No, I'm not," insisted Joni. However, the C-cup clearly didn't fit. The D did.

Joni cried in the fitting room for the next fifteen minutes, feeling as if she'd been turned into a porn star. When she saw her surgeon two days later so he could check the stitches, she blurted, "You gave me the wrong size! I'm a D!"

"I'm sorry," he'd said, "but I had to make a decision. The C did not look right from the way your skin hung.

You needed a little larger. Plus, it looks more balanced with your wide hips."

"I thought any size worked, even B's."

"No. A larger prosthetic worked—a decision made in surgery. I meant to tell you, and I'm so sorry I didn't," he said. "Your breasts do look beautiful."

The other downside was she could not feel the skin on her breasts. If Somi scrubbed too hard to cause an abrasion, Joni could not feel that. Matias and the men after him, however, had been pleased with her D-cup size. She got used to it.

Joni and Athena drank wine coolers in their towels on the roof above Koreatown. Athena was thrilled about Stewart.

"He sounds different from the others," Athena said. "I know Glen told me, but I forgot what Stewart teaches."

"Film something at USC."

"You don't know exactly?"

"All I know is I feel so—" She looked for the right word. "I'm *thrown* by him. It's like I can't think normally," and she looked off to imaginary stars. "It's like I'm lighter with him. Light-headed. I even feel happily lost. It unnerves me."

"Mom, you're in love!"

"No, no, that can't be. We haven't even slept together yet."

"Don't you want to be in love?"

"I want.... I don't know if it's attainable even. I don't want mere comfort or companionship. I want something more, something like twin candle flames in the dark!" She laughed. "Someone who speaks to my soul."

"Now you're talking," said Athena excitedly. "Maybe you've found him!"

"I'm not sure. I don't like being not sure. Frankly, I don't get how people fall in love time and again. I'm not built that way. I believe other people, but ... I don't know." She sighed.

Athena laughed and hugged her mother. "Mom, enjoy this. See where it goes."

Joni nodded, then looked at her daughter more sternly. "You recently compared me to Trump," said Joni, "which I didn't appreciate."

"I did? I don't remember." Athena smiled.

"You said I end a relationship the way Trump fired people on *The Apprentice*."

"I don't remember saying that exactly, but— Hmm," said Athena, as if not knowing how else to express what was on her mind.

"What are you thinking?" said Joni.

"It's just with Glen, I can tell him anything."

"Are you saying you can't with me?"

"You're not always easy, Mom. With Glen, I don't feel as if I'm in a swordfight!"

"Swordfight!"

"See what I mean?"

Joni stayed quiet.

"And, okay, now that I'm married, we're kind of equal now, right?"

Joni merely nodded.

"So I'll be open. Sex with Glen," Athena began.

God, no. Joni didn't want to hear about sex with Glen, but she had to at least pretend she was open to this, so she nodded. She and Athena never talked about sex the way Joni could with Kim. Kim could be bawdy. Joni didn't particularly like thinking her daughter was doing the nasty.

"Sometimes with Glen," Athena said, "I feel naked beyond naked. It's like he gets me. What I don't get is we can go on for hours. I mean, we might be drinking pinot grigio at sunset, fall into bed, and it's as if time stops. We take breaks every now and then for water, but, heck. Next thing I know, it's ten p.m."

Hours? Joni thought. What's the point? The right guy could get her to climax within ten minutes. Then again, that's about all Matias could go.

"It's crazy," said Athena. "Sometimes I feel addicted. Then I realize it's spiritual."

"Spiritual?"

"Really spiritual, Mom. I didn't think I could feel this with anyone. Maybe it won't last. Maybe two people can't keep this kind of thing going. What if in the future sex only goes a half hour—will I feel disappointed? I don't know, but I'm not going to worry about it now. I just wish you could find someone like Glen."

Joni smiled to herself. She'd never like someone like Glen. But Stewart—Stewart was different. She wondered how he was in bed.

Later that week, Joni followed the directions on her Google Maps and found Stewart's cute single-story house just off Linda Vista in the hills above the Rose Bowl. She never ventured over to this part of Pasadena, and Stewart assured her it was still Pasadena, as if being in Eagle Rock was somehow less.

After she locked her Jaguar, Joni adjusted her dress slightly so her cleavage didn't reveal too much in her low-cut dress. It was her killer dress, one she hoped would do the work.

"You're gorgeous," he said, after opening the door while she was still in the street. She walked through his front yard, a rose garden, to his porch. Joni had to step carefully on his flagstone walkway because she'd worn heels to make herself taller; he was so tall. He welcomed her in with a hug and a big kiss, which she wasn't prepared for, and it left her light-headed for a few seconds. Joni twisted one ankle and almost fell over, but he caught her.

She laughed. "Wow. That was a kiss."

He directed her into the kitchen where beautiful cherrywood cabinets stood with stunning granite countertops, accented with a blue-gray paint. Artichokes floated in a big pot, no flame beneath them yet. She'd never had artichokes before. "Gorgeous," she said, motioning to the whole kitchen. "Did you have an interior designer?"

"Sort of—my cousin's wife. She looked at photos when I was having it done. She was the one to suggest the granite and the dark paint."

He gave her a quick tour of his home, and Joni couldn't help but look at the place from her real-estate-agent perspective: real hardwood oak floors, nine-foot ceilings, one and three-quarters bathrooms, a back yard against a wooded hill, a redwood deck with a built-in barbecue, and one bedroom turned into an office, all great.

"Did you live here with your wife?" she asked, thinking the woman's ghost floated around.

"No. We'd lived in Beverly Hills. She bought my half, which got me this place. All new furniture, too."

The large dark sofas and the painting of an ancient Japanese warrior on one wall felt definitely masculine. Joni liked masculine.

The other bedroom, the master with a full bath that included a Jacuzzi tub, well, she wouldn't mind soaking in that.

"What is it you teach at USC again?" she asked.

"Filmic writing. Actually, that's the old name. Now it's called writing for the screen and television."

"Scriptwriting?"

"Yes, but it's more than that. People don't give enough credit to great screenplays, such as, say, Aaron Sorkin's *The Social Network* or, way before that, Robert Towne's *Chinatown*. The best writer of movies of all time? Preston Sturges."

"I don't know those writers."

"When we met, you mentioned *Game of Thrones*. That and all good TV and film reflect life, reveal life, show us new meanings, enlighten us, reveal a fresh path. It all starts with the script."

"What about directors? I always thought of film and TV as a director's thing."

"That's true. A good director paired with a great screenwriter, and you have a world view. That's why I have all of Kubrick's films. Same with Billy Wilder, Coen Brothers, Orson Welles, Buñuel, Malick, P.T. Anderson, and more."

Joni didn't recognize any of the names but said, "You like what you do—just like me."

"That's why we're alive, right? To find our purpose."

By his bedside, she spotted a pipe in the shape of an arm with the hand holding an urn, which was the pipe's bowl. Next to the pipe stood a little black bottle marked "The Green Earth Collective." That's where her daughter bought marijuana. Joni had been upset at first, discovering her daughter smoked, but Athena had said, "It's legal, Mom, and it's much better than drinking. Have you ever tried it?"

Joni hadn't, so she tried it with her daughter. One time, she smoked too much, and she hated how she felt just so weird because drinking a glass of water with ice felt special, magical, and so wet.

Joni lifted up the pipe, smelled, and laughed. "Don't tell me you as a professor smoke. Isn't that, I don't know, unethical—or at least unacademic?

"My dad grew up in the sixties, and I smoked with him as a teenager. It didn't make me less inquisitive—maybe more. Do you smoke?"

"Very little. Maybe a puff or two."

He patted the bed and they both sat. He rummaged in his nightstand drawer and pulled out what looked like a pen. "Have you ever vaped?"

"With my daughter once. I liked it—not as harsh as the buds she had."

He handed her the pen. She looked for the end with the hole, put the pen in her mouth, and drew in air. A blue light on the end came on as if it were a blue-burning cigarette. She didn't inhale a lot. She felt nothing. She took a little more and handed him the pen. As he used it, she exhaled and saw a light blue smoke come from her mouth. Joni took one more hit. He did too, offered it to her again, and she shook her head. He put the pen away.

"I thought we'd eat the artichokes first, then I'll barbecue the steak."

"You're treating me so well," she said, noticing then and there how truly handsome he was. He had a strong chin, great lips, and thick black eyebrows that she hadn't particularly noticed before. "Are you Russian?" she asked.

"You're good. Yes, my grandmother was Russian, so I'm one-quarter. Her father was a Russian Orthodox priest. And you?"

"Half Mexican. My father, an Argentinian, picked up my mother hitchhiking in Ensenada. She was just a teenager. He got her pregnant, so he moved her to a house next door, just outside Ensenada, and his wife let him. My mom had my brother, then had me, before my father's wife stabbed him to death in the middle of the night."

"Oh, my god." He touched her cheek compassionately. It felt good.

"My mother had an aunt in Chicago, so we moved there after that, when I was five. I later became a citizen."

Joni took his hand. He squeezed lightly.

"And you had Athena when you were a teenager?" he asked.

"Yeah, I ran away from home at sixteen. My mother had a series of violent boyfriends. I wasn't going to put up with her bullshit anymore. I don't regret any of it."

"Is your mother still alive?"

"Yeah, in Montebello. I see her maybe once a year."

She paused. She'd never told any man this story before. Shit. The pot was stronger than she'd thought. "It's not like I spend Thanksgiving with her," she said. She waved the topic off, not wanting to think any more about her mother, her black hole, and was about to stand, when Stewart leaned over and kissed her.

Kissing was like Roman arrows flying or a pack of dogs chasing a cat—lots of energy. She felt his desire, his breathing deeply, his rubbing the small of her back as they kissed, and she delighted in it. Soon her hand moved downward, and he did not resist. Joni flashed on the movie *Showgirls,* where Elizabeth Berkley liked to give lap dances to clothed men. That was laughable. This wasn't.

Before long, after slowly taking off each other's clothes, which just seemed so natural, they kissed, lying sideways, skin to skin. Rather than racing to his goal, he spent time with her. He was an attentive lover, taking things slowly when that was what she wanted and then fast for when she asked for that.

Her body rocked hard in an extreme spasm when things clicked just right.

"Are you okay?" he asked when that happened.

"Oh, yeah. It can hit me hard. I do think sex is important for a relationship."

"Me, too," he said.

Before Joni knew it, darkness wrapped around the room. They'd been making love for over an hour. She had climaxed twice. Was this, dare she say, *spiritual*? It wasn't as if she heard a voice or saw a deity. Joni hadn't needed a man like this before, though, and was that good? She put spirituality out of her mind. This was merely good sex. Very good sex.

"I didn't expect that," she said, her head against his chest, hearing his heartbeat.

"We didn't even get to the artichokes yet," Stewart said.

"I went for the steak," she said, laughing at her own joke.

They finally made it to the kitchen, each wearing a robe, and he whipped up hollandaise using whole eggs, Smart Balance margarine, and fresh lemons. As he continuously stirred with a whisk, he said, "My hollandaise is slightly different from traditional, but it's healthier. It took me a long time to find the right margarine to replace the butter. Whole eggs are better than just the yolks. And I really like it lemony."

He kept stirring over a low flame, and the yellow mixture started thickening. She'd never seen the sauce made before.

"How wonderful," Joni said. "I'm a fan of Eggs Benedict, and most of the time, the hollandaise isn't lemony enough."

He smiled and said, "You are one in a million."

At the table, she watched how he picked a leaf from the artichoke, dipped the tip in the hollandaise sauce, and scraped the soft pulp and hollandaise together with his teeth. She followed suit. The taste wasn't bad, not as "vegetably" as she expected. The sauce was great. When the leaves were gone, he showed her how to scrape off the "choke" as he called it and get to the heart. He'd figured out she was a beginner. He said, "The heart is everything."

After they finished, he said, "Ready for a steak and my great potato salad?"

"Can we wait a little?"

"Why?"

"I wouldn't mind if we went back in your bedroom."

"Where have you been all my life?" he asked, and they eagerly returned to the bedroom.

Joni did not focus on her real estate business as much over the next two months. She had been used to working most Saturdays and part of Sunday. She'd usually reserved Sunday afternoons for doing things with Athena, including now going to movies, which they did with Glen, too. Lately, she saw Stewart three to four times a week, usually staying at his place Friday and Saturday nights and doing things with him Sunday afternoons. Sometimes those things had him working on the Sunday *New York Times* crossword puzzle while she might read pending contracts or prepare her list of things to do during the week. "Sometimes" also included making love for hours. As it had for Athena, such long lovemaking seemed unusual, yet Joni lost herself in it. It felt like a high-wire act. In fact, some nights on her drive over, she hoped they'd rush to the bedroom. Was this what crack cocaine was like?

One time, a weeknight after she returned home at midnight from his place, she just had to write him an email, one that he'd read when he woke up.

Dear Stewart—

I had an amazing evening with you. In fact, I'm always amazed by our time together. Sometimes it doesn't feel real. I leave your place like I'm some space capsule floating above the equator. It's just pure bliss. Or is it just lust? Or is it lust at its best? Will this wear off? These thoughts, though, vanish as quickly as I think them because they trivialize our time together.

I love our pillow talk, enjoying hearing
your take on current events to
something one of your students said. I
love your slow and penetrating kisses.
You make me feel so at ease. You can
be critical about movies, but I never
feel critiqued. I can be wrapped in your
arms for hours, wondering if you can
read my mind, and a desire begins to
grow. I want to absorb you into my
cells, like alcohol. It's past two in the
morning. I count the hours until I see
you next.

Affectionately,
--J.

Stewart had two dinner parties over the next month
as if to show her off to his friends. He told her she could
invite Athena and Glen or any of her friends. Joni said
she'd rather hold off for now. Because he was cooking,
she found herself surrounded by his friends who asked
her questions. How long had she known him? Did she like
his humor? What's her favorite movie? Who was her favorite screenwriter?

For the last two questions, showing she'd learned
from him, she said, "*True Grit*, the new version, and the
Coen Brothers. They're my favorite writers, too."

Later that night after everyone was gone, during pillow talk, Stewart said, "You know what I like about you? I
can't predict you. I love your curiosity. You look at things
in an usual way—and you make me laugh all the time.
You were great with my friends."

She placed her hand on the back of his head, gently
pushing her fingertips into his dark hair. "You're hand-

some—and smart. Pardon me if I'm too direct, but I can't get enough of you. It worries me."

"Yikes," is all he said, and soon they were kissing and making love again.

Afterwards, after they regained their composure, he said, "I can come to your place, you know. I've never been inside. Are you messy?"

"No, no, it's nothing like that. You just have such a wonderful house. My one-bedroom apartment is rather Spartan." She'd moved into it after Athena had moved in with Glen.

"I'd have thought a real estate agent would have found a deal for herself."

"I owned a house when I was married," she said. "I just... I don't know. It's not important to me. A great office is. I love my office."

"You haven't invited me there, either," he said.

"I didn't know you were interested. I haven't been to USC, either, now that I think of it."

"We'll do each sometime," he said.

"Absolutely," she replied.

A few days later when they made love, as they each got into it and she was on top, feeling so good, eyes closed, blood rushing in her ears like the sound of hummingbird wings, he said, "What do you think of our taking a vacation together?"

"What?" The sound of his voice had some meaning, but she had to pause to consider.

"Where in the U.S. would you like to go? I have air miles I can use. Is there someplace you'd like to visit?"

He felt so good beneath her at that moment, and Joni wanted to go anywhere with this man. "How about New York City?"

"Yes!" he said. "We get to make love in all those different New York beds. Doesn't that sound incredible?"

"The best," she said.

"Plus, it'll be a real test of how we get along, don't you think? I think we'll do great."

In the pit of her stomach, anxiety grew. Why did he have to make this so "real?"

"Do you want to do AirBnB's or hotels?"

Now she could feel her breathing come faster. "Sorry," she said, getting off him. "I need some water." She drank from a nearby glass. So did he.

"What would you like to see in New York?" Stewart asked. "I think we should see the Empire State Building and the 9/11 Memorial for sure. Movies in the Village. Man, this could be a start of a lifetime of wonderful trips."

She gritted her teeth. "Could we talk about this later?" she said.

The next night, sleeping alone in her apartment, Joni woke up gasping. She just had had a most vivid dream. She and Matias had stood in a long line at a Blockbuster Video, a line that had snaked around the inside of the store. This had to be around 2008 when there were such stores. He was asking her about the two DVD movies he had, "Should we get *The Dark Knight* or *WALL-E?* One is funny, one is dark."

"I don't want either, really," she'd said. "Is this our life—a lifetime of movies?" She had been in line doing the *New York Times* crossword in pen, but she never did crosswords. Stewart did. That was odd. In the dream, she stood on her tiptoes to scan for Athena in the kids section. She found her in the action section with *True Grit* in her hands, the older one with John Wayne on the cover. Athena had to be ten.

"But you suggested this place. What do you want? And you pointed to both of these movies," said Matias, confused.

"Because they are popular. I don't care really. They'll probably bore me. Everything here will." He pulled out a jawbreaker sealed in cellophane from his coat and popped it in his mouth. Joni had said in the dream, "Those things can break a tooth."

"What do you want to do then?" he'd asked, paying no attention to her jawbreaker comment.

She had considered. "Athena is old enough to stay home. Let's go out drinking."

Awake in her bedroom, Joni remembered that she had really said that once to Matias. The pressures of her life were great then – lots going on at her job, and young Athena was becoming more assertive, and Matias just seemed so needy then. A few drinks could help them both. Was she the one to start him drinking? Was she the one to make him fall from grace? She was still breathing heavily.

Joni thought about finding Matias in his bedroom—which used to be their bedroom—slumped on the bed on a blood-soaked quilt, a shotgun at his side, and half his head missing. Joni had been glad that she'd made Athena stay outside on the front stoop when he hadn't answered the doorbell. After the coroner had taken his body away, but before the cleaning crew that specialized in blood removal had come, she'd found one of his teeth in a clean part of the carpet by the door. Had it ricocheted off the wall, which looked like a giant splatter art piece with some little holes? She should have called him the night before when he had made her promise she would. Still, it was his life. He was the one to take it. God damn it! Why did he have to do that?

She didn't see Stewart for three days after that dream, but then she received an email from him late one night.

Dear Joni—

I haven't heard from you in a few days.
This thought occurred to me after 10 p.m.
as I'm sitting in this bed, the very bed

we've had such delicious times in. I had
held off making love with you for a time
when it felt right, and we found that right
moment. I'm not often an insecure person,
but we all have our late nights, as it were,
and now I'm wondering did I write or say
something wrong, something insensitive?
We usually communicate every day.

You have not given me one sign that I
should be worried, other than I've noticed
neither of us has used the word "love," not
even in our notes. You like the word
"affectionately." I often use "Yours"
because I feel devoted to you.

Thinking about this has made me evaluate
how I feel. I hope you don't mind my
saying this, but I love you, Joni! You may
not feel the same yet, which is perfectly
fine. You're just taking me to places of the
soul I hadn't imagined. You have an
amazing spirit. Let's talk in the morning.

Love, Stewart.

When Joni read this, she found herself breathing
hard, and she knew she'd better write her thoughts down
while she had them. She wrote:

Dear Stewart,

Thank you for your note and courage. You
probably held your breath as you clicked on
Send. Truth be told, I found myself
hyperventilating after reading your last six

sentences again and again. I respect your feelings and have to explain things. I don't want us to be awkward with each other. I happen to think the word "love" just comes with so many parameters and expectations. Once couples start using it, things change, and not always for the better. Flaws get masked. Labels are made. It's as if we step into little boxes that our parents imagined for us when we were kids.

I want to continue this journey with you, talking, sharing, making love, bursting into laughter, disagreeing about films, learning about stories, passionately kissing, holding each other, snuggling, feeling your skin against mine, hearing your heart beat as I lay my head on your chest, smelling your wonderful scent. I'm worried that using charged words in the "getting to know you" phase will add pressure and make the good disappear.

I realized the other day that I see the world more brightly with you. Time stops somehow with you. We're like twin candle flames in the dark, illuminating. I care for you deeply. Is that okay? Can I come to your house today after work, the usual time? I can explain more then.

--Joni

Joni reread her note when she awoke just after six a.m., and she sent it. Within a half hour, Stewart wrote her back.

Joni—

Of course that's okay! I'm glad I brought the
word up and am happy to continue our
journey together. What I feel is magical. What
you wrote is so specific and personal, I can't
help but drink it in. Maybe we should use
Woody Allen's word he used in *Annie Hall*,
that he "luffed" Diane Keaton because the
word "love" just wasn't enough. Remember
that incredible shot where they sat by the
bridge in the evening? That was the
Queensboro Bridge from Sutton Place Park.
When we go to New York, maybe we can go
there and luff each other.

I'll use my own word to end this:

Lerfingly,
  Stewart

P.S. I feel like a note in a bottle, washed
ashore, and your sweet hands found my words
inside. See you tonight!

Joni arrived at his house at five-thirty as usual,
straight from work, wearing a red dress and low-heeled
shoes. She showered in the master bath, put on his robe
and applied her makeup. In her little travel bag, she'd run
out of Q-Tips. He must have some, so she looked in the
drawers beneath the two sinks. The third drawer held a
big pack of Q-tips. A small picture frame lay upside down
beside it.

Joni looked at the picture. Stewart and a pretty woman held their arms around each other, apparently on a

boat. The woman wore sunglasses; Stewart didn't, so he squinted. It must have been late afternoon. There wasn't enough of the boat or landmarks to show where they were. They looked happy. A long lock of the woman's dark hair came down across her face. The woman smiled brightly as if to say, "He's mine." Was this Stewart's ex-wife? Why was it in this drawer? It must still have meaning for him. Perhaps this was his sister. No, he didn't have a sister.

Still in the robe, Joni found Stewart in the kitchen, cutting onions, and she said, "I ran out of Q-Tips, so I used one of yours. Hope you don't mind."

"Of course not. Anything you find, you can use."

"I also found this." She handed him the picture, and then he looked at her, puzzled.

"It was next to the Q-Tips. People sometimes misplace things, so I thought maybe you misplaced this."

"I'd forgotten about this," he said.

"Is it your wife?"

"Yes. Miranda."

"She's pretty."

"She's a nice person."

She felt a pang in her stomach. "She must still mean a lot to you if you have her picture in your bathroom."

"No. Nothing to read into. I probably plopped it there when unpacking. Why?"

"Well, I mean before you, I'd dated some guys on Match, and it's surprising how many men explain their ex-wives were not affectionate, and that's why—"

"That's not the case, Joni. Is there something you want me to explain? I'm unclear."

"I just told myself I didn't want to get involved with someone with past-marriage issues or—"

"I don't have—"

"Like one guy I saw was only legally separated."

He looked shocked. "Is that what this is about? My legal separation?"

"You told me you were divorced. I was just giving that as an example."

"I am, in essence. Miranda and I went through divorce proceedings with a divorce mediator. A few days before we were to sign the papers, Miranda found that once she was divorced, she'd have to refinance the house because I'd no longer be on the deed. While the monthly mortgage was affordable for her, the bank told her she would not qualify for a re-fi—not enough income."

"Are you saying—"

"The lawyer explained a legal separation works exactly like a divorce. We did it so she could keep the house and pay me off."

She looked down. Joni worked on her breathing until she had the ocean. "It just seems you still have ties to her."

"What I have is the same as a divorce. She had to buy me out, and I'm not legally responsible for the house. It's in her name. The legal separation is the same as a divorce. Besides, I never see her. I've been truthful."

"This is just a surprise, is all."

"If I want a true divorce, all I have to do is pay forty dollars to the city, and my legal separation becomes a divorce. Is that what you want me to do? You don't like the word 'love,' but I love you. It's not a label. It's not a box. I'll pay the forty dollars if you like."

"No, I mean... no. It's fine. We're still getting to know each other is all."

"Are you okay?" Stewart asked.

"I'm not hungry," Joni said. "I don't know why I get like this. All I know is I like feeling you next to me in bed."

He led her by the hand to his bedroom where he sat her on the bed, and he plunked right next to her. When he put his arm around her, that only brought up the picture again with his arm around Miranda.

"I don't want anything to get in the way," he said. "Is there something more I can say?"

She shook her head. What she wanted was him, and she kissed him hard as if her molecules could meld into his. As the sun set, shadows moved across the walls, bats with belfries, tiger salmon on the river leaping up the rapids over boulders, and somewhere else on the globe, the sun rose, perhaps over a jungle with cicadas loud as carpenters. Incense burned for Buddha, and the lovemaking sang of guitars giving in to sweet surrender. Purple seemed the color of the day. Dream on, on to the heart of the sunrise.

"Are you okay?" he said again after she became quiet, her synapses firing like rockets. "We hardly got started."

"I'm fine," she said, even if Miranda's dark lock swung across her face. "I don't like losing myself."

"What do you mean?"

Joni said nothing. She did not know. They held each other for the longest time until it was fully dark. Joni said, "I have to go."

"Why? Don't you want dinner?"

"How about I come back in two days, and we'll try this again? You can make me dinner then."

"You sure?"

"Yeah. I'm just tired. It was a hard day."

"Okay." He flicked on a light. He looked like a stranger. Joni quickly dressed, and he put on the robe she had worn earlier. It was his robe. She stepped toward the door when he said, "Don't I get a hug?"

Joni hugged him, then drove home.

She couldn't sleep. Instead, she wrote Stewart an e-mail.

Stewart—

Tonight got me thinking, more than
usual. You brought up my definition of
love again, which made me ponder. I
sense you love Miranda. You're still tied
to her. You'd kept the information of
your legal separation from me, and
that's because you like that tie.

As we were in bed, I kept seeing that
picture of Miranda. Before she was an
abstraction for me, but the way you two
looked so happy. I can't imagine we'd
ever have a photo like that of us
together. You shouldn't have dated until
you had a real divorce even if that
meant she lost the house. Divorce is
about cutting all ties.

I'm sorry. I've really had great times
with you. Thank you for making the
time together so exceptional. This will
be the last communication you'll ever
get from me. It's best to be clean.

In truth,
    Joni

With that, she slept well. In the morning, her phone
rang, and she could see it was from Stewart. She didn't
answer. A half hour later, an email arrived from him. She
opened it. It began, "I am absolutely devastated. There's a
tragic misunderstanding here. Let me explain." Joni
didn't let him. She deleted the note before she read the
rest of it. This had to be clean.

A half hour later, she received a text from him that said, "Did you get my email or message on your phone? Please call. I'm sorry if I miscommunicated anything. We need to talk."

She did not call. Joni drove to work, smiled at Joyce, her secretary, nodded to others in the office, and concentrated on an offer for a house in the hills for one of her clients.

Joni received three more text messages over the next few hours from Stewart. One said, "It's normal for miscommunication to happen. To fix it, we need to talk. May I call you?" Minutes later, he tried calling again, so she just powered down her phone.

A half hour later, her office phone rang, but she let her secretary pick it up. Joyce said, "It's your daughter."

Joni lifted her receiver and said, "Hello, my dear."

"I just received a phone call from Stewart." The tone was stern—so unlike Athena.

Joni's heart fell. "You don't need to get involved," Joni said. She realized it had been dumb to date someone with ties to her daughter.

"He's trying to understand what's wrong. What's wrong, Mom?"

"Nothing. He's like some other men I've met. He really loves his ex-wife. He has divorce issues."

"He read me your note. Stewart said you have it totally wrong, Mom. What're you afraid of?"

"Don't take that tone of voice with me."

"I'm not a little kid anymore," said Athena. "And at this point, I'm worried about you. Here's a man who clearly cares for you, even loves you, and you shut him down. Why? Why so harshly?"

Joni tried a different approach. "Athena, my dear. Did he tell you he's not completely divorced?"

"You know he is. The fact a bank doesn't recognize it only means he's smart."

"I didn't mean for you to get involved. Stewart's nice, don't get me wrong—but it wasn't working. He's into movies, and I'm not. He likes cooking artichokes. Listen, I've appreciated you and Glen setting him up for me, and I truly thought this would work, but he has issues with his wife that he didn't tell you about. I'm sorry to involve you."

"I don't mind being involved. Is this something to do with Dad?"

"Your stepfather? Not that fucking psychology shit again."

"I'm happy to help."

Joni could see the opening and said, "You help me a lot, Athena. Maybe I don't credit you enough, but even finding Stewart for me, that was very nice."

"Really?"

"Really."

"Mom, we're here on earth to make relationships. It really takes two people to make it through the daily shit. That's why I have Glen."

"That's why I have you, honey."

Athena paused, then said, "Should I call Stewart back for you and explain whatever you want me to say?"

Joni truly did not want to talk with him ever again, so she said, "Sure. You can tell him about your stepfather, if you like. Even if I'm over that terrible incident, it's a good excuse. Just realize, I'm not a victim, Athena. I didn't raise you to be one, either. Tell him whatever. Wish him a good life."

"What if he comes to future family events?"

"We're adults, we'll be fine."

However, Joni started blubbering, and her eyes watered, and, God help her, was this going to turn into fucking tears?

"Mom, are you crying?"

Joni made it sound more like a cough, and, once she had her steady breathing back, said, "I must be getting a cold. I'm fine, dear. I'm meant to live alone. You and Glen move up to Seattle. I'll be fine."

There was a long pause. "Maybe we shouldn't. I don't want to abandon you."

"Honey, this is just life. We're really just parchment in bottles that have drifted ashore. The sand washes over us all."

"What are you talking about?"

"It's something Stewart said. Did you know the Milky Way has over a billion stars? What are we, just stardust?"

"Mom, are you okay?"

"Yeah. Are you up for a Korean scrub in the next few days?"

"Sure. Can I say—"

"We'll talk in Koreatown."

With that, Joni hung up, wiped her tears, and paced around the room, wondering how she let herself think she and Stewart were two candle flames in the dark? How absurd was that? Yet part of her felt as if she'd lost something. But what, really? She wasn't in control with him. She didn't get enough work done. Now things would be fine. She felt in control again.

Stewart wrote emails daily for a week, which she deleted. One more text came on a Sunday afternoon when he normally did his crossword. It said, "I give up. Have a good life."

That's what she expected to do. He contacted her no more.

That same Sunday, the curtains in her living room were drawn. The only furniture that stood in the room was a cotton-covered easy chair the color of burnt sienna, well worn, dependable, like someone who didn't drink or didn't play with guns. She plopped into it. Beneath the chair's threadbare cushion lay something she put there to remind her of things: a single tooth.

You Wreck Me, Baby

Two months after I'd helped her pack, near the end of the year and shortly after I received my wife Alexa's "good night" text from her new apartment across town, the one that didn't take pets, I herded our two dogs out for their evening constitutional. One dog, a scruffy terrier, took his time as usual, sniffing this rock and that plant. The other, a Cavalier King Charles, peed right on the sidewalk and then, with her big piquant eyes that melted my heart, demanded her biscuit.

Once I gave her one, her tail swished into allegro mode, and the other dog quickly did his business for his treat. Dogs have a simple life. Me, lately, I had had a hard time falling asleep, parsing where it all went wrong. Should I have not given Alexa a surprise birthday party last year? Should I have not taken the window seat with our last plane ride? Should I have not married someone whose name woke up Amazon's smart speaker?

On my walk back into the house, a dead, heavy palm frond plunged like a sword onto the ground somewhere behind me. I scanned the sky for the moon where the goddess Diana resided—no moon—and its absence felt as something more ripped out of me. The moon with its caring goddess represented assurance, nurturing, and safety. As I stepped onto my front entryway, I felt a sensation I hadn't for fourteen years: a sharp pain in my back. I knew what it was: a kidney stone, a corkscrew twisting into my body. "Of course!" I yelled into the air. This was the exclamation point to my eventful year.

In the previous summer, when the antibiotics for pneumonia did nothing after I'd coughed for three weeks already, my doctor referred me to a pulmonologist, and a CT scan found nodules in my lungs. He asked, "Have you ever smoked?" When I said no, he looked doubtful. So this was how I was going to die? Lung cancer? It happened this easily?

A biopsy took two weeks and showed it wasn't lung cancer. A rare syndrome, vasculitis, which inflamed my lungs' blood vessels, could have killed me if not diagnosed properly. Then, a few days after the powerful steroids I took kicked in, and I wasn't coughing anymore, Alexa left me. "Javier," she said. "It's nothing to do with you. It's me."

Sure.

Then she was gone.

Now this stone.

Having been through his before, I drank a lot of water right away to push the stone through, even if its coral fingers would scratch down my urethra. I tried a shower to decrease the pain and, heck, to look better if I had to go to the hospital. I found my hydrocodone pain pills for just a situation like this. I popped a couple and hunkered into bed, hoping the stone would disappear. From their circular beds next to me, the dogs stared at me in the dark as if they smelled anguish.

For two hours, I couldn't sleep. The pain dulled but I shivered violently. I had to yank on my winter coat and slip under the covers. I knew I couldn't avoid the hospital.

The next question was do I call Alexa or 911? While the reassuring hydrocodone would give me confidence to drive, it would subtract my ability, and I'd better not endanger others. Alexa was asleep already, and I knew a hospital visit would take all night. She didn't need to be miserable. I'd already made her that way.

I called 911 and asked for an ambulance. The woman who answered wanted to know why.

"I have a kidney stone."

"How do you know?" she said in the tone of an aggravated wife.

"I've had them before."

"Have you taken anything?"

"Why do you ask?"

"Because you're slurring."

"And I'm not driving," I said with precise enunciation. "The battery on this phone is nearly out." I looked. Twenty percent left. "It doesn't hold a charge as it once did."

"I am sending an ambulance," she said. I thanked her.

After I hung up, I turned to the beasts. "Well, doggies, I'm turning on the house alarm, so you'll be protected."

These days I spoke with the dogs as if they were people. Probably soon, I'd end up buying them vests and hats and telling the neighbors the cute things they did. Maybe I'd become the doggie guy, posting dog pictures on Facebook, daydreaming with them about cats named Trixie.

I walked outside to wait. A lone coyote howled. Otherwise, all was quiet. A siren approached in the distance. I hoped the driver wouldn't have it blaring up the hill and waking the neighbors, now that it was after midnight. Soon the siren stopped, and minutes later, a large growling engine moved in range, revealing a giant fire truck, red lights twirling. A fire truck? I wasn't on fire.

Four firemen in their big boots and florescent yellow jackets appeared before me, one opening the side of the truck and pulling out a case. "What's your name?" he asked.

"Javier O'Hara." I know, Irish last name, but my dad was Irish, and my mom from Peru.

He checked his clipboard and nodded. "How are you feeling?"

"You're the ambulance?"

"No. It's coming. I'd like to take your vital signs."

I smirked. He wouldn't find any.

"Let's go in the house." I opened it up to barking dogs. I turned off the screeching alarm. The man with the case asked me why they were called, and I told him of my back pain and suspected kidney stone. He took my blood pressure – 179/85 – and soon more red lights poured through the front door. The ambulance had arrived. Two young male paramedics in blue uniforms hurried in with a gurney on wheels.

"I don't need that," I said. "I can walk."

As I walked outside and approached the square-backed ambulance, one paramedic said, "Are you sure you don't want a gurney? You look a little wobbly."

"That's because I'm in pain. Get me to the hospital."

In the rear of the ambulance to Glendale Memorial Hospital, I sat sideways with a seatbelt. While one paramedic drove, the other sat in the back with me and poked at his tablet, then asked me, "How much water did you drink today?"

"I don't know. The usual."

"Which is?"

"Do coffee and energy drinks count?"

"Caffeine helps form stones," he pronounced. He was no moon goddess.

Through the tinted windows in the back doors, an array of parked cars slid past like the shells of people's lives. We arrived in twelve minutes. I'd later get a bill for

$1,200. I could have taken Uber for $12 and maybe received a few smiles.

At the hospital, after I had blood and urine taken for analysis, I was given a gown and told to put my clothing in a plastic bag they provided me. I sat like a prisoner in the hallway for perhaps twenty minutes alone, feeling forgotten, my plastic bag at my side. As a young woman in a pink uniform walked by, I stopped her. "What's happening?" I asked. "I feel abandoned."

"Would you like a mental health counselor?" She looked me up and down.

"No, I mean I have a kidney stone. Isn't anyone going to do anything?"

"About your feeling abandoned?"

"Can I get a shot? How about a pain shot?"

"Stay here. I'll ask."

Soon a male nurse pushed a gurney quickly toward me. "We have a room for you, sir," he said.

"And a shot?"

"The doctor will see you soon."

I climbed on the gurney with my bag, and he pushed me into a hallway marked "Cardiac Section" where there were hospital rooms.

"I don't have a heart problem," I said.

"It's the only room we have," he explained. I shared a room with an old man with Einstein hair. He grimaced and held his chest as I entered, gave a little gasp. His Armenian son and wife turned from the news program to look. My nurse went over to glance at a monitor and then said to him, "You hurt, sir?"

"The pain," he said.

"Me, too," I said.

"I'll tell the doctor for you both." He whisked out of there.

Soon, a short woman in a white coat and dark shoulder-length hair stepped in, quickly stepping to the old man first. "Are you hurting?" she asked.

"Yes," he said.

"Your blood pressure is better, but I'll have the nurse give you more aspirin."

Aspirin is all? God, she better give me something more than aspirin.

She came to me. The tag on her coat said Dr. Mohrbacher.

"How are you feeling?"

"Terrible," I blurted. "Like a knife is in my back." She took both her hands and gently pressed on my chest above my heart. "How's that feel?" she asked.

"I'm not here for my heart," I said, but she pressed harder, and "Ow" spit from me.

"Interesting," she said. She then had me roll on my side. "Left kidney or right?

"My left side," I said, and when she pressed there, I screamed.

"Definitely. Let's get you to ultrasound."

"And pain medication?" I asked.

"Soon," she said.

It didn't happen soon. I hobbled to the bathroom in pain, and as I peed, a rainbow of colors trickled from me, first brown, then red, then orange, then yellow, and then faster. As I let it out, it felt like someone's fingernails going down the inside of my penis. My jaw clamped like two fists pressing each other. There had to be an easier life.

After I slid back in bed with its kid-sized blanket, my roommate's son and wife watched news program after news program on the wall TV, all night long. I heard that two men were found shot to death in their car in a Los Angeles park. Barriers to stop heavy trucks had been installed along the Rose Parade route in Pasadena, and there would be bomb-sniffing dogs. A chunky supermodel—"Plus-sized" she was called—happily spoke about being on the cover of the new *Vogue*, saying, "In this life, you gotta be who you gotta be."

With my eyes closed, I asked myself: who do I gotta be?

My bed/gurney started to move. A tall bearded man in a white coat wheeled me off and into an elevator. It kept going down and down. Finally I said, "Where are we going to? Mordor?"

"Subbasement C." The doors finally opened. After pushing me through a door marked "Ultrasound," he jellied up my back and rolled the cold instrument over my skin.

"Are you finding anything?" I asked him. He stared at me, so I said, "I've had these before and the radiologist never tells me anything. I have to wait for a doctor, but does everything in my life have to be a mystery? You wear a white coat."

He laughed. "You have a kidney stone in your left kidney and another stone in your bladder. A report here"—he tapped a clipboard—"shows you have a urinary tract infection, too."

"What happens next?"

He smiled. "Your doctor will tell you."

"Sir," I heard a young woman's voice say, "I'm here for my breast exam."

He stepped away from me, and while I couldn't see him, I swore I heard kissing.

"The nurses will come to get you," he said before leaving.

"You're abandoning me?" I asked.

"We're all together on this earth."

The door swung closed. In minutes, I heard the sounds of lovemaking. What was going on? "Doctor? Nurse?" I said loudly. I struggled to get off my gurney, each movement a white-hot flash of pain. They hadn't given me anything yet, so all the pain pulsated across my body.

At that moment, three female nurses rushed in, wearing pink uniforms and black floppy doggie ears like my Cavalier. I could see the ears on headbands, the kind for Halloween.

"What's going on?" I demanded.

"You must stay on the gurney," one said. "Your kidney stone is made of a rare earth metal, the kind used in cell phone batteries. The Apple Corporation needs your stone."

"What?" The three of them forcibly pushed me on my back to the gurney.

"Stop it!" I shouted. "I hurt," and I could only scream from the pain in my back and chest.

"You are making this difficult," said the nurse, now tying one of my arms to the gurney, while another nurse was tying the other arm; the third, one of my feet. I thrashed as best I could, but each movement became searing pain, and I started crying. "You're killing me," I shouted. "You have such a simple life!"

"We love you," they said in chorus.

"Love is in the next room," I said. "Can't you hear?"

"That's not love," whispered the nurse closest to me. "It's just sex. What do you want?"

"Both," I said.

"You need to be alone for love. Your stone can wait."

Darkness. I was a brain floating in fog.

The next thing I knew, I was waking up back in my cardio room, the news from my roommate's TV wafting in once again. Something about an early morning crash on the 110 in the six o'clock hour.

I groaned, and the son looked over at me, and he said. "You feeling better?"

My hands were still tied to the gurney, and I struggled. I noticed I now had an IV, and it went into the crook of my left arm.

"Let me get someone," the son said.

Dr. Mohrbacher soon entered, saying, "Feeling better now?"

"Why am I tied up?"

"You're not going to be a problem?"

"What?"

She started undoing my restraints.

"It says on your chart you took hydrocodone before you came in. Is that all?"

"Yeah, just a couple. I have them on hand in case I ever had a kidney stone."

"You were quite agitated at one point."

"Those nurses with doggie ears forced this on me."

She glanced at me with a what-planet-was-I-from look. "That's why we couldn't give you pain meds. You seemed to have taken too many."

"What's in there?" I pointed to the IV bottle and moved my arms and legs, now that they were free.

"Antibiotics," she said. "For your UTI."

"In the past, I've had saline to push out the stone."

"Your stone is too big, wedged into your kidney. It's not going anywhere now. Is the pain all gone?"

I had to take stock. It was. "Wow. Yeah."

"I'm going to check you out and give you a prescription for antibiotics. You'll have to go to your regular doctor to see what to do from here."

"Surgery?"

"There are a few options. Call your doctor later today."

"Always a mystery," I said.

"Do you have someone who can pick you up? We won't let you take a taxi or Uber."

"I can call my wife."

She frowned, then looked on her chart. "You're not married, it says."

"I won't be soon. She's a good person. She'll pick me up." The doctor nodded and left.

I found my phone in my pants by the bedside. It showed seven percent battery. Good. I could still call.

It was almost 6:30 a.m. I imagined the dogs waking up and finding I wasn't there to take them out to pee. Their urinary tracts, stone-free, should have filled. They would see the empty bed of their owners and probably pee on the floor. I called Alexa.

"Hello?" said her sleepy voice.

"Sorry I woke you," I said. "I have a favor to ask—about the dogs. Could you take them for their morning duties? I'm in Glendale Memorial Hospital."

"You're in the hospital! Why?"

"Kidney stone."

"Why didn't you call me? Why why why didn't you call me?"

"Because you moved out. That's the point, right?"

"You know I care for you."

"You do?"

"Christ, this is our problem. You don't connect."

"I'm trying."

"We have to make a promise to each other. If either of one of us has to go to the hospital, we will call the other. Yes? Promise?"

"I promise."

Just then, a pink-uniformed nurse without doggie ears came in with a sheath of papers in hand. "You're discharged," she said. Alexa heard and said, "I'm coming to get you."

Twenty minutes later my cellphone vibrated. Alexa's picture showed up on my phone, a photo I'd taken of her at Laguna Beach two happy years ago with the sun highlighting her shoulder-length auburn hair, her eyes bright, loving. Alexa said, "I'm in the lobby."

"I'm paying my co-pay. Be there soon."

When I found the lobby, Alexa sat sleepy-eyed, looking out into the new gray day. Her profile made my heart leap. She was a tall woman with a slim figure. We'd spent fourteen mostly lovely years together. Couldn't we just be ourselves, be who we gotta be, love each other, help each other through this often-unforgiving world? We arrived at this point because we never argued? "People argue," said our marriage counselor. "Life brings up problems. If you don't disagree at least every few weeks, something's wrong. Javier, that should have been your clue." *Please, Alexa,* I thought. *I'll argue. I'll make you steam.*

Alexa drove me home to what used to be her home, to the house we had selected and bought together. It sat on a hill with a view of Griffith Observatory in far-off Hollywood. I wish I'd been a better observatory. As I glanced at her driving, it occurred to me that we had both loved each other deeply. I had felt her love. She hadn't felt enough of mine. Just because you send a message doesn't mean it's received.

The dogs took turns jumping on our legs, happy to see us. After the dogs' morning ablutions outside, I asked Alexa, "May I make you breakfast?"

In the past, she'd felt it was her job to cook. She was the wife. She'd always said, "I have to be good for something." She had a whole list of responsibilities for herself that included cleaning the whole house, doing all the laundry, cooking, and making half our income, something her mother did. Were we each merely a sum of the people of our pasts? What seeped into me from Alexa?

"Yes," she said. "Breakfast would be lovely."

"Would it?"

"Why?"

"Just trying to argue."

She rolled her eyes.

I'd shopped only the day before: thick low-sodium bacon, jumbo eggs that I'd scramble, and a fresh rustic baguette.

I used four eggs, added a little water, and stirred vigorously. In the frying pan, the eggs thickened, becoming soft and fluffy. I microwaved the bacon, which became crisp the way Alexa liked it. I toasted the baguette, and made 100% Kona coffee, my recent indulgence. One has to have such things when abandoned.

When I sat down next to Alexa, she took my hand. "Thank you," she said.

"No, thank you for coming to rescue me." The warmth of her hand gave me hope. I needed it.

"I'm not sure how much of a rescuer I am," she said. "We're so different."

"All couples have gaps. Everyone's different."

"Are you talking me out of what I feel?"

"No." I paused before saying, "Is this an argument?"

"Hardly."

At that point, she placed her bacon on top of her baguette, just as I had, which she had never done before. We ate that way together.

Alexa stood to leave after breakfast. The Cavalier peered from the couch, her cute doggie ears reminding me of my night. I glanced at Alexa, who was staring at me and then looked away. At the door, Alexa and I kissed. I knew then she wouldn't be back, but we loved each other.

In the months that followed, I'd have kidney stone surgery, with Alexa by my side. Then after that, she wanted to keep living alone, and we'd divorce. She'd get a new place that allowed pets, and she would take the dogs for occasional visits. She didn't want too many responsibilities.

Right at this moment, though, after Alexa left, both dogs looked at me with hopeful eyes. It occurred to me life isn't the movies. Sometimes we get surprised, and that's that.

"No worry," I told them. "I'll give you biscuits."

The dogs stood against my legs, tails wagging, mouths trying to speak. I petted them simultaneously. A young couple ran by and waved to me.

7 *Truths about Love*

P hysicists know about potential energy. A rock balancing on the edge of a roof has much potential energy. So does a person rejected in love.

Melissa heard a rustling in the bushes just after Roy, her estranged husband, left the doorstep of her rented West Covina, California, house on Christmas morning. He had stopped by to give a gift, a stuffed bear, to their little girl.

Melissa waited until she heard his car drive off before going to investigate.

"Where Mama going?" said two-year-old Steph. "Where Daddy?"

"Daddy's gone. I'm just getting the mail, honey. Stay here."

Melissa spotted the Christmas wrapping in the bushes first, then the forty-ounce bag of Starbucks coffee she'd given him as a nice gesture. So much for that. The more she thought of it, though, it pissed her off. He was the one to have an affair with her boss, the young Mrs. Tananger. Despite his denials—oh, there was much evidence, such as his trip to Catalina Island and the empty condom wrapper in his pocket—Melissa moved herself, her daughter, and most of the furniture out one day. They moved into the house she had rented while he was at work. He had yelled into his cellphone at her when he came home, demanding they come back, which only confirmed she'd made the right decision.

Roy taught English at Mt. San Antonio College in the nearby town of Walnut. Melissa worked in the college's IT department, which is how she'd met Roy, fixing his desktop computer. At their wedding, Roy met her boss, Brooke Tananger, and Brooke's husband.

A year after Roy and Melissa married, Melissa gave birth to Stephanie. While Melissa was nursing, he was off with his new friend, Brooke Tananger, hiking on one of their many excursions. "It's just hiking," he would say. "You don't like to do it."

That's when the affair began, Melissa had guessed. She complained to Human Resources that her boss was bonking her husband. The director did nothing. However, everyone in IT knew about Brooke and Roy. The days rolled by. When H.R. did nothing about Brooke and Roy, Melissa quit her job and moved. She found a better job keeping the PCs running at Cal State L.A. Brooke, that bitch, divorced and moved in with Roy. Roy divorced Melissa. Melissa's gift to Roy, coffee, was her trying to accept everything.

Now she was really mad. Her heart beat rapidly and her hands shook. How could she get him back for ruining her life? She'd thought of how he had complained about her cats, that she had been a crazy cat lady, and he had insisted her cats become outdoor ones. One by one, they were eaten by coyotes. When he was angry with her, he would clean his rifle in the easy chair facing her in front of the bed. She wished he could feel just as helpless and intimidated as she had.

Then it struck her. She'd heard of something on the radio called swatting—very illegal. It was calling the police falsely to say someone had a gun and was pointing it at someone. The SWAT team then might bash in the door and show up, guns drawn. Just the thought of Roy being startled and holding up his arms to a team of police pointing guns at him made her smile.

Love is like a great Hollandaise sauce. Cooking it right is in the details.

Melissa had to be careful and not get caught, especially since Roy would claim she must have done the swatting. She reconsidered. She could lose custody of Stephanie doing something like this.

Her brain offered, "How about I use a payphone?" That could work. But where were payphones anymore? The Shell station on Palmetto Avenue had one, she remembered, not far from his house that he now shared with the newly divorced Brooke Tananger. Melissa had to do this. She knew Roy thought of her as weak. She would be weak no more.

At her next gas-up, she used the Shell station, and she casually looked around. She spotted a camera focused on the pumps. The payphone would be in the deep background—a risky thing. Better not do it.

Two days later, a Saturday, Melissa took Stephanie to a Goodwill store to buy her bigger clothes. Steph was growing so fast, and Roy wasn't giving her any money for her care. In fact, in the coming week, they had to go to court to battle over that issue, and he wanted joint custody. At Goodwill, she spotted a dark red hoodie with USC emblazoned on the chest. A hoodie...

That night, with Stephanie in her child seat in the center of the back seat, Melissa parked her car in the back of the Shell station and said, "Mama will be right back."

She walked toward the front, drawing up the hood of her USC hoodie. There on the side of the station, before she got in range of the camera, she took a few deep breaths and ran in place as fast as she could so she'd be short of breath. Then she ran quickly to the phone, as if she'd been running for blocks on adrenaline. The sign next to it said an emergency call to 911 was free. She dialed 911.

"Nine one one," said a female operator. "What is your emergency?"

She spit out in a higher voice than usual, "My husband tried to shoot me! I ran out, but he has a gun! My mother and daughter are there! Please help!"

"What kind of gun?"

"What kind of gun? Really? It's long. With bullets."

"What is the address, ma'am?"

Melissa gave Roy's address. The operator said to please hold, but Melissa said no, she's going back. She hung up and ran back to her car.

"Where did you go, Mama?" said Stephanie, content in her seat.

"I just needed change."

"What's change?"

"Money. We needed different money," Melissa said, and started the car.

Look at a person's quirks. Multiply by five.

The clock radio came on in the morning to the usual National Public Radio station. Approaching the top of the hour, when there was local news, the local host Chery Glaser said, "A West Covina man was shot last night by police in response to an emergency call. In an apparently false phone report, the caller said the man was holding two people hostage with a gun. The police department is investigating." According to an anonymous source, when the police shouted to the man who answered the door to hold up his hands, he reached for his back pocket—apparently for his wallet. There was no word on his condition at County USC Medical Center.

Melissa turned off the radio and shook. Did she just kill Roy? In no way did she intend that. He was the father of her daughter. The jerk was supposed to hold up his hands. Leave it to him to do things his way.

She woke Stephanie and dressed and fed her. Melissa drank coffee. Her stomach churned. The coffee's acid wasn't helping.

"What's wrong, Mama?" asked Steph.

"I have an upset tummy."

"I can kiss it."

"You're a very sweet girl. I love you so much."

"How much?"

"Taller than this house."

"I love you taller than the trees!" Steph laughed.

Melissa dropped Stephanie off at daycare. One hour into work, the police called her. Detective Bento introduced himself. Her heart instantly dropped. She'd expected a call, but not this fast.

"What can I do for you, Detective?"

"Are you aware your husband was shot last night?"

She gasped. "Shot! Who shot him? Why? Is he okay? He lives in a good neighborhood. Did he shoot back? He's got guns."

"What kind of guns?"

"Pistols. A rifle. How bad was he shot?"

"He's in critical condition at County USC—an accidental police shooting. He's awake. He suggested you might have made a false call to 911."

"A false call? Why?" To herself, she sounded quite surprised.

"We have a 911 recording from a woman saying a man was holding his family hostage. She gave his address."

"Why would Roy hold anyone hostage? From whom?" Roy had always corrected her when she had used "who" incorrectly.

"That's what we're trying to find out. Did he have enemies?"

"He could piss people off. He pissed me off, but I'd say basically he's a good guy. We're divorcing as you probably know, but he's the father of my child."

"So you can think of no one who had it in for him?"

"He's a college English professor. He gave F's liberally. Maybe some angry student had something out for him."

"I hadn't thought of that."

"Ah," is all she said.

"Swatting tends to be a young person's thing," he replied. "They think it's funny."

"Ah," she said again, noting his pronoun. If Melissa had said "a young person, they," in front of Roy, he would have stopped her, pointing out that "a young person" is singular, and "they" is plural. Pronouns must always match.

We are fragile creatures with the delicate bones of a bat. Find a lover who understands that.

Melissa and Stephanie visited Roy in the hospital, a typical room in beige with bright fluorescent light. Already sitting and with white bandaging encasing his head, Roy smiled when they walked in. His normally handsome face appeared puffy with bruising under one eye. Wearing one of those terrible hospital gowns, he also held an arm in a sling. Melissa noticed all the flowers in vases around the room and was glad she didn't buy him flowers— gladder still not to see Brooke.

"Daddy!" Stephanie yelled happily and ran to him. "What on your head?" she asked. Melissa lifted her onto the bed. Roy held his daughter with his one good arm.

"I have... a few... owies," he said slowly. Something was wrong with his voice.

"We're so sorry to hear," said Melissa. "I would never wish this on you. I hope you know." She handed him a rectangular present wrapped in the Christmas paper she still had.

"It's coffee!" shouted Steph.

"Can you... open it for me?" said Roy.

Stephanie tore into it as if it were her birthday. Then she held out the box of Trader Joe's Instant. "Coffee!" she again said proudly.

"It comes in individual packs," said Melissa, "with sugar and creamer in it already. I know how much you like coffee." Neither of them mentioned her previous gift to him that he'd thrown in the bushes.

"Thank you," he said appreciatively, and the way he looked at her, he meant it. Maybe if he were shot every day, he'd be a good person.

"Why does Daddy talk funny?" Stephanie said, looking at her mother.

"The owie in... my head," said Roy.

Both of Melissa's hands started to shake, and she felt bad, as if the grim reaper was scything her from the inside, so she sat in the nearby chair. Brooke had probably sat in it most of the time. Were Brooke's germs attacking her now?

"Is Brooke okay?" said Melissa. "She wasn't shot, was she?"

"No, but it really... shook her up. She's called in sick. For the week."

"You don't have to talk," said Melissa.

"I worry... about her," he said. "Something like this— you see what... is important." Roy squeezed his daughter.

You're important," said Roy. He looked straight at Melissa next. "You, too. I wasn't... sleeping with Brooke before you moved."

"You don't have to talk," Melissa repeated.

He nodded.

A good relationship gets messy, like a chocolate bar left in a hot car. If it doesn't get messy, you're doing something wrong.

Over the next few days, Melissa found herself extremely lethargic. She figured it was depression, but one morning, her hands were shaking, and her heart was beating so rapidly, she thought she might die. Was she about to have a heart attack out of guilt? He would get Stephanie full-time. She called a friend to come babysit. Melissa drove to Urgent Care to get checked out. She'd told the doctor about her husband's shooting, saying it worried her. After listening to her heart, feeling the base of her neck, and looking into her eyes with a scope, he said he wanted to do a few blood tests.

"For what?" she asked.

"Before your husband's shooting, had you been under stress?"

She laughed. "I'm in the middle of a divorce. Before that, he was cheating on me."

"Do you exercise? Belong to a gym?"

"Not with a two-year-old, a full-time job, and all this stress."

"Exercise is good for stress—and for keeping your metabolism working."

He asked more questions, including about her menstrual cycle, and said, "These tests will confirm what I think you have: Grave's Disease."

"Disease? Graves?" she whispered.

"It's not as bad as it sounds. Your thyroid regulates your body. We don't know what triggers it, but Grave's Disease is an immune system disorder where your thyroid produces too much in terms of hormones. Once I confirm this, medication can regulate it. You'll get your energy and regular cycle back. You'll feel much better about yourself."

A day later, the doctor called to confirm his diagnosis. "Tell me the pharmacy you use, and I'll call in your prescriptions."

Sure enough, by the end of the week, she was feeling much better. No more rapid heart beating or shaky hands. After a month, she felt better than she had for most of her adult life. Taking care of Stephanie was no longer a challenge but rather lovely, as if the souls of ten puppies swirled within the little girl.

One day, Melissa received a call from Caron Lee-Lewis, vice-president of academic affairs at Mt. San Antonio College, her previous employer. Ms. Lee-Lewis explained, "We have an opening you might like. Brooke Tananger, your old boss, quit a while back to take care of her fiancé." Apparently, Ms. Lee-Lewis did not know the fiancé was Melissa's ex-husband. "Now, many months later, the directorship is still open. You came recommended. I'm calling to see if you might apply for the job."

It would be a huge promotion. Melissa applied, and after two interviews and a few weeks, she landed the job.

Roy was no longer on campus. As he recuperated, he had applied for better positions, something he'd always meant to do. After he had applied to USC, not only did he get it, thanks to being in the news, but he was also made director of undergraduate studies. As he told Melissa (and he spoke to her much more kindly now), "No one really likes being in administration. It's more work for not a lot of extra pay, but I'm paid much more than I was at Mt. SAC."

Melissa became part of regular managers/directors meetings. When she walked into her first meeting, with only a few minutes to go, ten chairs were taken, leaving only the head of the table and a seat next to a tall man with thick long white hair in a ponytail. He looked like a young beardless Saruman out of *The Lord of the Rings*. He wore a gray jacket as a professor might wear, but over a black T-shirt. Except for his white hair, he looked to be in his forties. She sat next to him.

The man smiled at her. "I'm Stanislaus Blake-Lara, director of the International Students Program."

"Nice to meet you," she said, shaking his proffered hand. "I'm Melissa Mendicino—I mean, Grant."

"You're not sure?" he asked.

"I'm still not used to my maiden name again."

"Ohhhh," he said, nodding as if he now had a secret. "You used to be married to Roy Mendicino, the English professor—the one who got shot by police."

She nodded. All conversation at the table stopped, and ten heads, like fish with gaping mouths, now stared at her.

"Yes," she said. "And he has a lawsuit against the police. He'll probably get very rich." Wasn't that ironic, she thought. He had a better job, more pay, with a huge settlement coming in. Then again, she was better off, too.

At that moment, Caron Lee-Lewis, vice-president of academic affairs, entered, short, with bobbed hair like an ice skater. The meeting began with Ms. Lee-Lewis introducing her. "Melissa is the replacement for Brooke, and we're more than thrilled to have her here." Everyone clapped, as friendly as Christmas.

At the end of the meeting, Stanislaus Blake-Lara held the glass door open for her, his long freak-flag-hair flying. "May I walk you to your office?" he asked, and before receiving an answer said, "I loved your explanation that in tech help, people should not feel stupid about computers—that too many things in computing, such as interfaces, are not intuitive."

"It's true."

"I've felt stupid with some techies. I sense I won't with you."

"Thank you. I liked your approach, too—that international students are great observers of our culture, and you learn a lot from them, such as how our politics are crazy."

They chatted about the importance of a diverse student population. They soon reached her door, and she said, "Here we are."

"Would you like to go out to dinner this week?" he asked. She must have looked puzzled or surprised because he added, "There's so much more about being a director you might like to know. You're new to this, right?"

"Yes, I am. Dinner. Yes," she said, before thinking it through. His offer had actually made her tingle. "I'll have to see if a friend can babysit."

After he left, she sat at her desk with her door closed. She wondered: would he like Stephanie? Would he make a good daddy? Did he have a nice house? She shivered, realizing she was galloping ahead. Did she really need a partner? Real life just didn't make any more sense than dreaming.

She couldn't think like this. Time to focus. She had to arrange for computer repair.

Falling in love is like getting your teeth cleaned. There's the terror, a lot of poking and prodding, and then you come out with a better smile.

On the evening of the dinner, Melissa had severe doubts. She obsessed over what to wear and decided on a print dress and black high heels. The doorbell rang. Her friend Rena from Guatemala stood at the door, there to watch Steph.

"Look at you, girl!" said Rena, gray hair and Spanish accent. Stephanie came running from the kitchen and right into the arms of Rena, who kneeled to Stephanie's level. Rena grinned at Melissa and said, "You, too, Mel. You're stunning."

"What're we doing tonight?" Steph asked Rena.

"We can play moon puppets," said Rena.

"What's that? Or let's go swimming!" said Steph.

"Where? You don't have a pool. Don't be silly."

"You be Spongebob and I'll be Squidward."

"Run off and get into your pajamas," said Rena, and Stephanie pumped her arms and ran off.

Rena carried a stylish white leather handbag, one of the many she designed and sold. That's how she and Melissa met originally, at a flea market where Rena sold her bags. Now shops carried her purses. She handed it to Melissa. "This is a gift. It's lucky. Carry it tonight."

Melissa hugged the bag but stared at the floor.

"What's wrong?" asked Rena.

"I'm nervous. I shouldn't be dating."

"Of course you should. Who doesn't deserve a relationship more than you?"

"What if he's like Roy? I always fall for the domineering type."

"From what you said, this guy sounds like an old hippie. Try him out. Kiss him."

"What?"

"Your lips won't wear out."

Out in the driveway, just as Melissa sat in her car, her phone buzzed with a text. It was from Stanislaus and read, "I'm leaving in a few minutes. I look forward to seeing you again. You're a tall drink of water."

Melissa hyperventilated. Roy used to call her that, a tall drink of water. Where the hell did that phrase come from? Why couldn't she be a tall Coke or maybe a Mountain Dew?

She drummed her fingers. She texted him, "Baby sitter flaked out. Let's reschedule. Sorry." She rested her forehead against the steering wheel. Her plan was to never reschedule. She drove off to the nearest Starbucks, drank two tall Frappuccinos over two hours, and considered why she couldn't be a tall Frappuccino.

"How was it?" said Rena when she returned.

"I had a great time. I probably won't see him again, though. Not my type."

Rena frowned. "What type is he? I found him magical if he can be in two places at once."

"What're you talking about?"

"He showed up here with Chinese takeout. He said you'd texted him that the babysitter flaked out."

"I just couldn't—"

"He said he was originally going to pick you up here, but instead you said you'd meet him at the restaurant. He texted you that he'd bring food over."

Melissa looked at her phone. Indeed, there was a text back that she hadn't noticed.

"We called, too. You didn't answer. We had a great time," Rena said, pointing to empty boxes of Chinese food on the table. "We kept thinking you'd show up."

"Sorry about that."

"What were you thinking? He's a nice man. Funny."

"I don't have room for nice in my life right now."

They left it at that.

The next morning, her desk held a vase of flowers, delivered from a local nursery. She read the card. "Sorry we missed you. Stephanie and Rena are both wonderful. Don't feel bad. I've had cold feet before, too. Stan."

She found herself grinning, but no, this was not the time for dating. This guy just needed to be told the truth. She found his number in the school directory and dialed.

"Hello, this is Stanislaus Blake-Lara," she heard. "I'm away from my desk, but please leave a message."

She felt better she didn't have to talk in person and said, "Thank you for the flowers. They are gorgeous. They're brightening my day. However, my divorce papers only came through a few months ago. I really shouldn't be dating."

"Oh, that's too bad," said Stanislaus. "I really think we could have a good meal."

Flustered, she said, "Stanislaus?"

"You can call me Stan."

"I thought this was voice mail."

"Just messing with you. I have an odd sense of humor. So you like the flowers?"

"Yes."

"And I like your kid and your friend. How about lunch today? It's just lunch. If you don't like me, we'll just remain colleagues."

"Can I... I mean... You're nice, but I have lunch plans already. I think we should just stay colleagues. I'm sorry. I'm... damaged goods."

"You are not—and there's nothing to be sorry about. I can empathize. I divorced ten years ago. It took me a while."

Did he have any meaningful relationships in that period? Did they go sour? How did he get through his first year? She caught herself. She couldn't ask these questions if she didn't want to encourage him. She said, "Thank you. Not just for the flowers but the food you brought to Rena and Stephanie."

"You're welcome."

"See. I'm not what you call your ideal date. I'm a little quirky—probably something my husband hated in me."

"Don't be hard on yourself. I'll see you around the quad. You're okay, Melissa."

"Thanks," and they hung up.

The universe sometimes has funny ways of working.

A week later, Melissa picked up Stephanie from day-care, and Melissa had to return to school to get a laptop that she had meant to bring home for testing.

"I want soup, Mama," said Stephanie from her child seat in the back.

"Remember that Vietnamese soup I got you once? *Fuh?* It's pronounced *fuh.*"

"Fuh," said Stephanie.

"Yes, I got it from a restaurant near campus. We'll stop there."

Soon they arrived at Pho Hai, a simple little place with black booths, white walls, and black-and-white tile. As Melissa ordered two pho to go, Stephanie tugged on Melissa's blouse. "Mama. Man." Stephanie pointed, and Stanislaus sat in another booth, slurping from his giant ceramic bowl of pho with chopsticks.

"Stephanie!" said Stanislaus. The little girl ran over, and Melissa left her credit card on the counter to pay for the soup and followed.

"So we meet again," said Stanislaus, giving Stephanie a high five.

"Why you eat soup with sticks?" asked Stephanie.

"These are called chopsticks. This is the way the Vietnamese do it. You eat the rice noodles and meat first by pinching with the sticks, and then with this—" He raised a stubby Vietnamese soup spoon. "You drink the liquid with this."

"I like forks!" said Stephanie.

"You like a spoon," said her mother, and smiled. "Nice to see you again, Stan. Do you come here often?"

"A lot. I never eat on campus. I need to get away, especially when I work late like this."

"How long have you worked at Mt. SAC?"

"Twenty-one years. I started in the Office of Marketing and Communications writing press releases."

"Interesting."

"Then I transferred to the International Students Program and worked my way up. And you? You studied computer science?"

"Some. I started getting into computers in high school."

The tug on her blouse came again. "Soup, Mama." Stephanie pointed to the counter.

"You can join me here, if you like," he said.

"I'm sorry. We have to get home. That's why it's take-out."

"Another time, then."

As Melissa walked out with the paper bag of pho in containers in one hand, and Stephanie's hand in her other, she said, "Bye, Stan."

"You're something," he said.

In the car on the drive home, Melissa sighed. He did seem nice. She imagined kissing him. Would she hold his ponytail? But she knew she'd probably kiss with too much saliva or then say something wrong or worry about Stephanie, and, Jesus, why couldn't she be more comfortable with people? Men. Maybe she wasn't designed for this. At least with computers, there was logic.

Love is about surprise. It's nothing that comes in a Cracker Jack's box. It's more like a stumble in the street, and someone catches you.

The next afternoon at lunch, Melissa wondered if Stan was eating at Pho Hai again. Should she go there? No, a pizza would do at the Mountie Café, the food spot on campus. She simply had to stay focused.

The cavernous, high-ceilinged café buzzed with students when she entered, and most of the white plastic chairs were taken. She'd look for an open table after she got her pizza. As she approached the pizza area, she slipped on a spot on the tiled floor near the counter. Was it cheese? A young woman with a blue baseball cap asked what she wanted, and Melissa said, "There's a slippery spot right over—" As she turned to point, she heard the word "Shit!" and saw a man plummet, ponytail flying. His head hit the ground with a thump.

"Stan!" and she fell to her knees, dropping her white purse on the ground. She looked right at him, into his blue eyes as he tried to focus.

"I saw you come in here, and—"

"Shh, shh. Are you okay?"

"I just wanted to say hi. Why does this have to happen to me?"

Two blue-baseball-capped young women slid in next to her, each saying, "Are you okay?"

"Call an ambulance!" said Melissa.

"No," said Stan, "This is embarrassing."

"You hit your head. It's nothing to mess with. People are fragile."

She grabbed her cellphone from her purse as things weren't happening fast enough.

"Nine-one-one," said a female operator. "What is your emergency?"

Melissa's heart surged. Was this the same operator from last year? The voice sounded the same. "A man slipped on some cheese and fell in the Mt. SAC cafeteria. He hit his head. We need an ambulance."

"Cheese? Is that what you said?"

"Yes. Pizza cheese. It's a café... Mozzarella, maybe. The bigger point is he hit his head."

"Which café?"

"The Mountie Café, the only one here. Surely your paramedics must know Mt. SAC."

"One moment. Let me put you on hold."

Stan tried to push himself up, but Melissa said, "No, stay down. Let me feel your neck, see if it's tender. At least, that's what I saw on a hospital show once. I love those shows."

He nodded. "Me, too."

She lightly touched his neck. "Does your neck feel sore?"

"That feels nice."

"I'm sorry."

"Nothing to apologize for. Synapses are sparking. Electrons are colliding."

"I think you're getting delusional."

"Your touch is like a hummingbird kiss," Stan said.

She caressed his cheeks with the back of her hand, lovely man, saying "That's sweet." This was so unlike her, she thought. She was in foreign territory. What was she doing?

The 911 operator then said, "An ambulance is on its way. With whom am I speaking?"

Again, Melissa's heart surged. Would they compare her voice to the swatting voice? So be it. "Melissa Grant. I'm the director of technical services at Mt. SAC. The injured party is Stanislaus Blake-Lara, a very good man."

"Will you go with me in the ambulance?" he asked.

"Yes," she said. "Of course."

Two paramedics soon arrived. They carried a gurney.

The back of the square ambulance swallowed them all, Melissa, too, carrying her lucky white purse. Melissa and Stan soon whisked off into the afternoon, holding hands. This is how galaxies are made.

Jerry with a Twist

J erry lay twisted on his bed as if God had turned him into a frog's leg, ready to leap. He worried about many things—about their bills, about the birth of his son due in a few weeks—what if the boy comes out deformed or otherwise damaged?—and about the dent he made in his car door in a parking lot.

"Honey, are you okay?" His girlfriend, Cheryl, shook him, and he groaned. "Wake up," she said. "Time for your audition."

The audition! Now he could worry about that.

He dressed in his serious casual clothes—khaki pants, loafers, and a long-sleeve pin-striped blue shirt—not the black—that he'd ironed the night before. One shouldn't wear a suit for an audition unless perhaps it was for an elegant role, such as the psychiatrist in *Equus* or C.S. Lewis in *Shadowlands*, both of which he'd performed in college. One couldn't be in long shorts and sandals unless it was for a teenage boy, which he no longer was.

"I have a feeling you'll get it," said Cheryl in the kitchen at the drippy sink. He still had to fix that stupid thing. The landlord should, but he knew the landlord wouldn't, not with the stabilized Santa Monica rent. He'd learned that with the broken toilet. Jerry just wanted to—errrrr!—make it already, get away from broken anythings, and grab his life.

"I'm off," he said.

"Without your breakfast burrito?" Cheryl pointed to the one she made with scrambled eggs, fresh parsley, and hash browns, just the way he liked. It seemed she was making up for their recent lack of intimacy through food. She had spotted last month, and they freaked out, thinking it was a miscarriage. The doctor said everything was fine but no more sex until after the birth. He missed their time together—just one more thing making him tense these days. Still, her health was everything, even if she looked so sexy and swollen in her blue robe, her hair slightly askew—but he'd wait.

He ate half his burrito. "I just gotta go."

"Okay," she said. "Know that I believe in you."

He smiled as best he could, but once out of the apartment, he shook his head. She "believed in him." That wasn't enough to quell another huge worry: how much longer could he endure his dead-end job at Office Max? His boss, Stacy, always let him take time off for auditions, but she told him recently she wanted to promote him to assistant manager, replacing the last one who gave his notice by yelling at the front door, "I quit this fucking place!"

"A promotion means more devotion," she said. "I need you. Actors out here are more plentiful than our pens."

He liked their Tūl pens, the blue, not the black.

Stacy also said, "And no more New Zealand accent. It creeps me out."

"It's good, though," he said in his down-under accent. "Recently some New Zealanders asked me where I was from. I said Auckland, though I've never been below the equator in my life."

"So you're good. How's it help me?"

"People remember me," he said, back to normal. "It's good for business."

She considered, nodded, and said, "Okay. What the heck. I like you. Plus, you have a business mind. I want to make this the number one store in L.A. So you'll do it?"

"Let me think about it," he said, praying that he'd get his break soon, five years out of college. While a promotion might at least let him match Cheryl's income as a receptionist at St. John's hospital, he wanted to be an actor. He was born to act. That and a Tūl pen were worth about a buck.

He'd made a name for himself in Los Angeles's 99-seat theatres, which supposedly led to bigger, well-paying gigs. Still, great notices in the *L.A. Weekly* for his roles in Chekhov's *The Seagull* and Ronald Ribman's *Cold Storage* and a great review in the *Los Angeles Times* for David Rabe's *Hurlyburly* got him precisely nowhere. He was paid five dollars a performance because these little theatres barely squeaked by. No movie producers called him up. Rather, his agent pushed him for this commercial. If he didn't get this, he'd probably lose his agent.

In a building much closer than the Santa Monica office park where all the studio stuff was, he studied the script he was given before the audition, sharing a waiting room with three other actors. One was a balding, hefty guy in his fifties with a gray beard and round, black glasses. He looked confident, glanced at his script, and then soon read an old *People* from the coffee table.

"I've seen you somewhere," Jerry told the man. He hadn't, but it was a great way to get an actor talking.

"I doubt you have," said the man. "I've been a graphic artist most of my life and only discovered acting recently. A casting agent saw me singing in a barbershop quartet. She suggested I test for her, and it worked out."

"As easy as that?" said Jerry.

"At first acting was a whim, but I needed a life change. It's been great. I've shot four commercials this month, and soon they'll be airing."

"But no plays or films?"

"I've been cast for an indie. We'll see how that goes."

The other guy was more Jerry's age, taller, handsomer, but as he was reading, squinting as if he needed glasses, his lips moved. He was the first in, and within minutes he came out and told Jerry, "They want to see you." The actor looked sad. He must have flubbed it somehow.

Jerry walked in knowing the audition really started at the door. He had to appear as if this were fun, like going into Victoria's Secret last year with Cheryl and picking out revealing nighties—which is probably what led to impassioned congress in the parking garage and her accidentally getting pregnant. The room featured a long folding table with a man in his mid-thirties sitting at the center, looking neither exhausted nor welcoming. That had to be the director. Two slightly older women flanked him, one of whom looked pleased. That happy person had to be the casting agent, Lonnie Weintraub, who'd suggested his audition after his agent called her. Jerry's headshot lay before the man. Two leather easy chairs stood in front of the table, and in one sat a young woman in her twenties with lipstick as red as a fire hydrant and an innocent Anne Hathaway smile.

"I'm Roger Bennett, the director," said the man. "This is Lonnie—", pointing to his left, "—and my assistant Bernadette," pointing to his right. The director nodded toward the young woman in the chair near Jerry, saying, "And Holly Oatfield is our leading lady."

Holly extended her hand and said, "Pleased to meet you. I saw you in *Hurlyburly* a few years ago somewhere in the Valley."

"Oh, yeah. That was fun. Glad you could make it."

"You were great," she said, and her eyes meant it. She was rather sexy, too, two buttons on her white blouse undone. He didn't know her, but what a great way for an audition to start.

"Have a seat," said the director. "Mind if I ask you a few questions?"

"Go ahead."

"You've had some great parts," said Roger. "A little young for Willy Loman—"

"That's college but—"

"And some more substantial roles in L.A. theatre including the Rabe play."

"Thanks."

"But it doesn't look like a lot of film work."

"I did take Seymour Brown's 'Acting for the Camera' class last year. I'm totally comfortable in front of a camera." He didn't say that he had hoped for a feature film to start, maybe Spiderman's brother or some other superhero thing that would elevate his status. Still, this little piece of poo thing was a step forward. It didn't take a lot of great acting.

"Any questions about the role?" said the director.

"I'm her boyfriend," said Jerry, indicating the young lady. Jerry knew, though, you should always have a question to show your interest and to get interactive, so he asked, "About my last line?"

"Yes?" said the director.

The women looked at their scripts. Lonnie said, "Tampons?"

"Is that the way I say it, as if I didn't know what they were? Or is it more like 'Tampons?' as if it's the last thing in the world I expected?"

The director smiled. "It's just a Target commercial," he said. "Don't read into it too deeply. It's just supposed to be funny."

"Ah, like, tampons! What flavor?"

The man laughed, but all the women cringed. "Sorry," Jerry said, and breaking into his New Zealand accent, "I'm bloody sorry. Drinkin' too much Steinlager."

Now everyone looked confused.

"Let's do a run-through," said the director.

He and Holly started, and, staying in his normal voice, he quickly felt the part of Holly's boyfriend. Ostensibly, they were shopping in a Target store, and every item she asked him for seemed suggestive. They performed, smoldering, steaming. She stared right into his eyes. If subtext were aluminum siding, they were cladding a castle. He came to the last line. "Tampons," he said, not as a question, but as proof of his loyalty.

The director and two women all looked at each other, surprised.

"That was..." said the director.

"Yes, it's..." said Lonnie.

"Hot" said the assistant, but the director looked puzzled. He gazed at the script a moment as if trying to understand something. Then he barely glanced at Jerry and said, "Thanks. We'll call you."

"Thank you," said Jerry, knowing nobody ever called.

The director hadn't shouted, "Loved it!" or "You nailed it" or "We'll call your agent within the hour—you're it." What happened? Holly held out her hand. He shook and could feel a piece of paper go into his palm.

"Nice meeting you all," said Jerry, and he stepped out, trying to appear as sure of himself as he could.

"Tell the last guy he can come in," said the director.

Once he was in the hallway, he checked his palm. A little slip of paper had the words, "Hang around. We can have coffee after the next guy." He smiled. At least he wowed Holly. He felt instantly guilty. His girlfriend was pregnant, yet he'd been excited about this young woman. Not good. Then again, it could be innocent. Just coffee. Get away from the tension.

Jerry turned to the bald, bearded fellow and said, "They asked for you to go in."

"Thanks," said the guy, who got up and walked as if popping into a jellybean store.

Why would the director even consider that old dude? The old man couldn't be her boyfriend. Maybe he was the perverted Uncle who lived in the basement, ready to drag his niece downstairs by the hair. Quite soon, however, laughter erupted from the room, male and female together. Jerry moved closer to listen. The last line came as if tampons were a newly discovered engineering feat. The director clapped as he said, "You nailed it."

What's wrong with the director? Didn't he have eyes? Jerry felt defeated, like a crayon abandoned on a hot sidewalk. He left. He didn't want to deal with Holly. One woman was enough.

As he slinked to his car, he considered what a betrayal having his talent was. In middle school, his teachers had understood his gift, and he nabbed the leads in the plays. High school and college pushed him further. He had voice lessons and learned sound and light design and even directing. After his BFA in theatre, Los Angeles brought him some great plays to perform. Now he realized life can show you that you're good at something, then crushes you when other people with less talent, less focus, scoot ahead.

For him, acting was about revealing truth, and he thought he'd done that in his scene with Holly. Still, he didn't really want to sell products, and that probably showed. Is that what life was, convincing people to buy stuff they didn't need? Buy and then you die? He wanted to act to encourage people that life was worth living. What a joke that really was, though. Now it wasn't worth living.

When he arrived at his car, an eighteen-year-old Chrysler Sebring convertible—something sporty that he had before he met Cheryl, but it needed a paint job the way the West needed water—it did not start. Little click sounds came from the engine. It was either the battery or something really expensive in the electrical system. Errrr!

His phone was a brick—no charge. He needed to walk two miles toward home. Soon he spotted a young woman on roller skates and just a bikini and headphones, dance skating down the sidewalk toward the pier. This happened as he stepped off the curb, and not only did he twist his ankle, he fell into a muddy curbside stream of water. He shouted. "Hell! We're in a drought!" as if he could get other citizens outraged at illegal water wasting.

As he stood up, the side of his khakis and his blue shirt were now all muddy. As he tried to brush it off, he only smeared and made it worse. He limped toward home.

"Five dollars," said some scraggily bearded homeless man whose shorts and button-down shirt still looked neater than his.

"Like I've got five dollars just hanging around!" said Jerry perhaps too angrily.

"Sorry," said the man. "I just thought you could use it." The man slapped five dollars into Jerry's palm, the same one that had held Holly's note earlier that hour. The man stepped to his green Jaguar. Ah, so I'm the homeless man, thought Jerry. Frickin' day.

In the next block, Jerry limped down the pier to an old-fashioned ice-cream stand he knew. He needed just one good thing.

As he stood in line, he heard, "Jerry? Jerry, is that you?" in a sexy husky voice he knew too well, even though he hadn't heard it in five years.

He turned to see Rosa, the first girlfriend he'd had in Los Angeles after he'd returned from college in Denver. She'd had a car when he didn't. At the time, she also had a bank account, a job, and great clothes, all the things he didn't have. She saw him perform in David Mamet's *Sexual Perversity in Chicago,* and they'd become a little perverse that same night. Now, her cascading dark blond hair acted as parentheses to her bright smile and the curves of her low-cut dress. She'd grown even more beautiful since he last saw her. Her silver necklace showed the elegance she'd always had, and she licked mint chip ice cream on an old-fashioned cone with that wonderful tongue of hers.

"Rosa," he said, realizing too late that he revealed his one muddy edge.

"Wow," she said half-frowning, half-laughing.

"Just had a strange accident up there," he said, pointing up the pier to the road.

"Are you okay?"

She held onto the hand of a thin four-year-old boy. In his other hand, his left, the boy grasped a chocolate cone that dripped over his fingers. He moved behind his mother's purple print skirt and looked at Jerry warily.

"Oh," said Jerry, looking more closely, noticing the boy with longish blond hair had the same infuriating cowlick on his crown as he had had as a kid, like an exploding dandelion. Now that Jerry thought of it, the kid had the same quizzical expression he'd had in a photo his mother used to keep.

"This is Jeremiah," said Rosa.

Jeremiah? Jerry calculated. Maybe she'd stop taking the pill then. Is that why she was here? What was going on? Stay cool, stay cool.

"Hi, I'm Gerald," said Jerry, bending down, wanting to emphasize their names were really different. Jerry held out his hand to Jeremiah. The kid reached with his drippy left hand as if to pass off the cone. Jerry, too, was left-handed.

"No, that's okay. You keep it. It looks good."

The kid licked with delight.

Jerry straightened up. "So are you married?" he asked Rosa.

"I was," she said, "to his father, a film producer." She gave a name he recognized. That guy was old—or he had been until he'd died last year. In fact, he knew the man had lived north of Montana Avenue, the really rich area that butted up against the Riviera Country Club.

"Sorry to hear of his passing," said Jerry.

"Circle of life," she said, finishing the last of her own cone with a bite. She crunched and swallowed. "And you're married." It was a statement as she pointed to the ring on his left hand.

"Technically we're not, but we gave each other rings, and Cheryl is due with our first baby next month." He smiled, thinking about it. He realized her pregnancy was such a pleasant picture, he might use the memory in acting. Like Marlon Brando, he believed in method acting, first popularized by Stanislavski in Russia—the same man who'd directed and performed in Chekhov's *The Seagull* in the play's first great production in 1898 in Moscow. Jerry always researched his roles deeply.

"You'll like fatherhood," Rosa said. "I always thought you'd make a good dad if you could only get serious."

"I got serious."

"Still acting?"

He remembered her attitude now. She always thought he'd "get real" and put aside acting as one did croquet or badminton. He sighed. "I don't know if I'll keep acting."

Right then, little Jeremiah's chocolate scoop hit the ground, splatting partially on one of his green sneakers. His face immediately registered his horror.

"It's okay, it's okay," said Rosa, kneeling down to her son, racing in with a napkin from her purse. "Shhh," she told him assuredly, and Jerry couldn't tell if little Jeremiah would cry or not. He was right on the edge.

Jerry said, "It's okay."

She expertly scooped up the remaining ice cream and deftly tossed it in the nearby trash can. She then wiped off the brown from boy's shoe. "How about we walk down to the beach? You can wash your hands in the surf. How's that?"

The boy smiled and dashed for the staircase down to the beach.

"Jeremiah!" she screamed. "You wait for me." The boy stopped, antsy.

"Good to see you," said Rosa to Jerry, and then she and her boy raced off.

She'd been fun and funny when he knew her—but she didn't believe in his dream. She'd wanted him to move in—and more, he knew. At the time, he couldn't support her nor fit into her mold, and he knew he had to focus on his career. He'd told her they had "no more magic"—a line from the Mamet play. He'd been callous, he now realized. Still, things seemed to have worked out for her.

Jerry twisted back to the ice cream line, managing to step on the exact spot where Jeremiah had lost his scoop of chocolate. As he slipped and fell, Jerry knew he was under some kind of curse. He landed hard on his butt, and he thought he heard a crack.

A half-hour later, he limped onto the lawn of his apartment complex that overlooked Santa Monica Bay. Would he be okay for work tomorrow? Should he go to the doctor? Should he take the promotion? Was it time to give up acting?

He sat on the grass. Exhausted, he lay down and stared up at the clouds. Normally, the sky would be completely blue or completely cloudy—the marine layer, as Fritz the weatherman called it. The marine layer would burn away to show the blue. Today, however, small sharp clouds like daggers hung over him.

People don't get what they want, Jerry realized. That's why celebrities are celebrated—they're the few to get their dreams. When they do something human—stupid or bad like Lindsay Lohan or Bill Cosby—we hate them and cheer. We're glad for it. Let them feel what the rest of us feel: what it's like to not get what's wanted.

Except Cheryl did. She got pregnant.

At the screech of a seagull, he turned his head to watch it alight on a lamppost. Above the gull, more than a dozen white birds flew. Doves, he thought. They seemed like a pod of angels, swooping around in a circle-8 pattern, in and out of the palm trees, flight as regular as a pendulum. They were one unit, and when they curved one way, they became gray pixels. These birds did what they were meant to do. As the doves swooped around, the sunlight caught them, and for a moment, they were an arrowhead, all white. Wordless. Wonderful. He'd seen them before. One of his neighbors, he suspected, had raised them.

He wasn't ready to go upstairs and tell Cheryl everything that'd happened to him. He'd stay. Was this the moment that someone running with scissors would trip in an apartment above, and the scissors would sail out the window and land in his chest? So be it. The sun felt warm on his face, and he closed his eyes.

Minutes later, he felt the sun go out. Panicked, he opened his eyes to see the silhouette of a woman above him. The woman had an aura around her shoulder-length hair, hair he knew and often smelled and intertwined with kisses. He also recognized the posture and the arc of pregnancy.

"Cheryl," he said. "You're back from the store?"

"Yeah," she said. "You okay?"

"Why wouldn't I be?"

"I got you Thomas's English muffins. I know you wanted Bay's, but they were out."

"You can't always get what you want."

She nodded, mumbling "Rolling Stones," and sat next to him as if to reassure him he'd be okay. Women were good at that kind of thing. He wasn't sure what men were good at. Probably nothing unless you were old and gray-bearded and took acting on a whim. He flashed on the end of a performance he saw recently of Arthur Miller's final play, *The Price,* which was hardly ever produced but should be. In the play, two brothers, a doctor and a policeman, wrangle over what to do with the furniture they just inherited and the price for it. They argue, thanks to a lack of connection over the years. Even though the poorer brother, the policeman, doesn't reconnect with his brother, the policeman seems unusually upbeat in the end and reconnects with his wife. It's there in the subtext. The man knows there's nothing he can do but enjoy what he has.

Cheryl placed Jerry's hand on her belly. He felt movement, a kind of twisting. This was a funny kind of life.

Moxie

"What's the deal!" shouted the young woman, a pantsuited executive, looking for dents on her silver BMW the way a surgeon searched for gallstones.

"I didn't see," said Martin in the parking lot at Vons, pointing to the rear window of his sporty red-and-black Mini Cooper S. "I have a narrow window. I just didn't see you."

"God! Didn't your drunken mother give you eyes?" spit the white-collared woman.

His wife, Samantha, never talked to him like this. Sometimes she didn't talk much, but certainly never rudely.

Martin, who worked at the Jet Propulsion Lab, joined the woman at the front of the BMW and pointed to a particular spot on the woman's bumper. He stayed calm. "I hit you about here. See, there's no damage." Martin pointed to the rear of his Mini Cooper. "No damage there, either. We're both fine. The God you speak of gave you plastic bumpers, right? As the man in *The Graduate* told Dustin Hoffman, 'plastics.'"

The young woman, easily half Martin's age, stared at Martin as if he were a low-level employee. "What the hell are you talking about? There are certain expectations we have in society," she said, "and no one needs to be broad-sided."

"I'm sorry," said Martin. "For your troubles, may I buy you some fried chicken?"

The young woman frowned as if he were insane, marched into her still-running car, revved the engine as if to emphasize its BMWness, and screeched off.

Martin had zipped to Vons grocery store to buy himself dinner, fried chicken, because Samantha had left to meet a girlfriend, forgetting to cook for him. She still must be feeling poorly. As he considered this, his eyes widened. While he was here, he could get Samantha some surprising thing that might turn her around. She loved ice cream.

He now deliberated over the many choices of frozen desserts. He'd settled on Ben and Jerry's Empower Mint. That should show her he cared. Should he call her? Weeks earlier, he'd forgotten to call her from the store to see if she needed anything. When he returned home, she'd said, "Do I even equate in your life? I just don't get this. Why do I have to go back to the store when you could have called me? You've got to include me in this relationship while it lasts."

While it lasts? he'd thought to himself. "I'm sorry," he'd said.

He couldn't call. She was in some elegant restaurant. However, what if ice cream weren't enough? He bought her twenty pounds of cat litter, too.

As Martin drove home, up a steep hill, he passed a dead orange tabby cat—poor critter, never saw whatever hit it from behind. Just over the cat and up the hill bloomed a waterfall of ground cover bursting with pink flowers. Martin often sat on his back porch, near his perfuming white jasmine, and breathed in the beauty of the near and distant flora. White and pink against an azure sky. Right now, though, driving, he felt uneasy, as if a deep bass chord played in his mind.

What was it about Samantha? Perhaps he shouldn't have gone to an all-boys high school. Perhaps he had learned about women and the language of love at too late an age so that he had a funny accent. His romantic gestures, such as giving her her own checking account, could come across like dry ice bouncing on water, fizzing and smoking away. So what might be going on with Samantha? Was it clinical depression again? Martin knew he wasn't the best caregiver, but he tried to emulate her. After all, when he had pneumonia earlier in the year, she had brought him mint tea, would sit with him for hours, would cuddle him in bed at night. When she felt down, however, she always preferred being alone, so he didn't know what to do. Ice cream and cat litter might help.

Maybe it was about sex. The love they'd made in Denver and most of the year had felt perfunctory. He didn't talk to her about it, of course. Sex was a dangerous territory, and she'd already said a few times that her body just wasn't cooperating anymore.

"I'm fat," she'd said in Denver. But she wasn't. As if she knew what he was thinking, she grabbed some skin on her belly and pulled. "Fat."

Honest and wide-eyed, he'd said, "You're beautiful."

Their trip to Denver had been a delightful surprise. When someone in the University of Denver's advancement department discovered Martin, an alumnus, worked at the Jet Propulsion Laboratory in Pasadena, looking for life on Mars, they invited him and Samantha to come to Homecoming Weekend in October, all expenses paid. They asked him to speak to alumni in a giant tent on the quad during that weekend, and he also met with a few science classes in Boetcher Auditorium, the stadium-seating classroom where he'd once taken physics classes. With Samantha by his side, he told the new generation about his JPL science team—different from the engineering team. These days, they focused on developing MOXIE, a new instrument designed to pull oxygen from Mars's carbon dioxide atmosphere. The name was an acronym for Mars Oxygen In-Situ Resources Utilization Experiment.

"If you saw the movie *The Martian,*" he'd told the alumni and students, "that's exactly how they got oxygen, breaking it from the carbon dioxide atmosphere. The thing is, we still have to create that device for a manned mission. My team is inventing a small version, which will be the proof of the principle on the next rover in 2020."

Samantha, unusually quiet on the trip, had never been to Denver. As they walked in the center of campus by the colonnaded Anderson Academic Commons, he said, "Memories race at me from every angle. I can picture my younger self running around, loving college. I wish I'd known you then. Then we'd have these memories together."

"I was only eight when you were eighteen," she said. "You'd have bought me ice cream cones and Keds."

"You're right. Still, this place makes me feel connected to you."

"I don't feel connected," she said. She'd throw these zingers at him occasionally as if to shake his tree. One time, seven years into their marriage, she'd said, "I've never been in a relationship that's lasted seven years. I don't know if I can do it." He'd replied, "Watch it go to ten," and laughed. They just needed to enjoy each other, and they had. They'd made it to lucky thirteen.

Even so, he took this connection comment seriously. *Something* was going on. Ever since their daughter—his stepdaughter, technically—left for college last month, Macalaster in St. Paul, Samantha hadn't been herself. She'd been much more withdrawn. The empty nest thing. He celebrated that they could do more traveling now and be spontaneous with each other. Samantha seemed focused on what she didn't have.

Rather than talk directly about it, he had said in Denver, "Sam, let's do a touristy thing this morning. Let me take you to the Red Rocks Amphitheatre."

"Whatever for?"

"It's outside of town in the foothills—known for its rock concerts. The Beatles played there in 1964. A riot at a Jethro Tull concert in the seventies closed it down for a while. I saw Judy Collins sing there. Want to go? Give us some new memories."

"Memories," she said as if the word were a favorite torn-up T-shirt. She pulled on a small smile. She was trying.

On the way to Red Rocks, Martin said, "I see you're down. I'm guessing it's about Julianne in college."

"It's not so simple," said Samantha.

"I'm here for you if you need me."

She nodded and remained quiet.

They climbed the sixty stairs from the parking lot to the top of the amphitheater. The open-air performance space was tucked in between giant red walls of dramatically angled sedimentary rock. To fill the silence, he said, "This is where I first knew I loved science. How could something as amazing as this be formed?"

Her long auburn hair rustled across her face in the wind.

He pointed to the wall of rock to one side. "This is part of what was called the Fountain Formation from the Paleozoic era. Three hundred million years—give or take a few million years. This is what's left of the ancestral Rocky Mountains."

They found themselves breathing hard by the time they arrived at the plaza at the top. A mile-high altitude can do that, Martin thought. Or was it his sixty years and Sam's asthma?

"You like to talk," she said.

"I guess I do."

He stopped talking. It occurred to him only then that Red Rocks appeared very Martian-like.

They walked to the far edge of the plaza to where the semicircular bench-seating started, dropping down to a stage nestled against a wall of red rock. Their spot offered a spectacular view of greater Denver in the distance. When he had been in college, the view had been all rocky soil leading to the flat plains and then Denver beyond. Now a huge housing development lay just beyond the park. A white SUV drove into the driveway of a huge, boxy house with a red roof.

"Want to walk to the stage?" asked Martin.

Samantha shook her head. "I need to breathe." Again she gave a short smile.

"Okay."

College-age kids in jogging outfits ran up and down the stairs. In his day, they'd have worn jeans spattered with paint and perhaps a ripped T-shirt.

A pair of young women in tight spandex ran across one level of seats, then down to the next level. A young bearded man with a mat performed yoga to the side. This place was a gym for these people. Martin left Samantha sitting on the top row while he climbed down the stairs. When he turned back, she looked off in the distance as if seeing something he couldn't.

As he came up to her from below, he felt lucky. Her beautiful hair, thin frame, and those wide hips remained inviting. How could something as amazing as Samantha have been formed? Focusing on her with his new digital camera, he said, "Hey, you!"

Cocking her head, she gave him a dour look. Then her face softened. "I love you, you know," she said.

And with her guard let down, she smiled. That became the one great photo from their trip. Earlier in their marriage, she had smiled at him often with unabashed glee. When had that changed?

The sex they'd had in their Denver hotel wasn't bad, as he reconsidered. Frankly, he remained amazed, thankful he could still do it. No one he knew had explained sex in one's sixties to him with the exception of his father. His father, survivor of a heart attack, eighty-six and living in Sonoma in the wine country, had said that married women—Martin's mother, for instance—tended to "accommodate"—quick sex to fulfill their husband's needs. He said women didn't particularly like it after their child-bearing years. Martin wondered if that were true. Samantha often initiated it.

His father's last sex had been twenty years earlier when he had been sixty-six, and Martin's mother, according to his father, "was done with it."

"Too much info, Dad," Martin said at the time. Now Martin wondered what Samantha felt during sex? She never liked talking about it beyond "You seemed to get off." She was a very private person. That's all he could say.

After he and Samantha returned from Denver, he said, "That trip was great. We just need to get away more often. Do you realize we haven't taken a vacation of any sort for four years?"

"Yes," she said, with her plastic gloves on, holding a small, lined wastebasket and a blue pooper scooper. She was about to clean the four cat boxes on the two levels of their hillside house.

"You keep working extra at Hummingbird Garden," he said, referring to the Pasadena preschool she worked at, not far from Caltech. "We don't need the money."

"I like working. It gives me purpose."

"Our lives together are a purpose, too. Our spirits need to be fed, just like our animals." They had five cats because Samantha liked cats. The deal in owning so many was she had to be responsible for the cat boxes. "We need time for ourselves," he said.

"You don't have to yell."

"I'm not yelling, Sam. I'm … sorry." He left it at that.

When he returned with the ice cream, Samantha was still out, so he made himself a chicken pot pie, high in sodium, which his doctor would hate, but Martin wanted convenience. Samantha always kept track of his sodium, saying he didn't want a heart attack as his father had, did he? Samantha had gone out to dinner with one of her few friends, Mirabelle, who worked at a funeral home as a reconstruction specialist. Someone had to do that, he supposed. He hoped Mirabelle could talk with Samantha in a way that Samantha couldn't talk with him, tell Samantha she needed to travel with her husband to share more of her life.

As he tried to find a new show on Netflix, a Danish detective series his colleague Dr. Volpe had mentioned, the lock on the front door turned. Samantha walked in.

"Hey," he said, swinging around on the brown leather couch. "Just in time. Want to watch a new Netflix series?"

"Not really," she said. "Can we talk?"

"I bought you a surprise," he said. He yanked himself off the couch and strode to the freezer. He handed her the pint of Ben and Jerry's.

Bewildered, taken off track, she blinked at the container. "I've never heard of this flavor. You know I like vanilla."

"I thought you'd like something new."

"Okay," she said, handing it back to him. He returned it to the freezer.

She moved onto the leather couch in the living room, and he followed. She appeared serious, shaky, as if she'd witnessed an avalanche. "What?" he said. Had someone died? Or was something wrong with her friend Mirabelle?

Samantha laid her small silver purse on the coffee table, grimacing.

"What's wrong?" he asked.

"This has nothing to do with you," she began as she sat down next to him and faced him."

"What?"

"I need to leave. I just need my own place—perhaps just for a little while."

"Is this a joke? It's not very funny." He looked her in the eyes, her beautiful green eyes. She once had mentioned to him that he didn't look at her when he spoke. She preferred eye contact. He looked. She seemed serious and near tears.

"It's just so I can get stronger, find out what I want," she said.

"What you want? I thought you wanted us. Did I hear you right? You want to leave?"

She nodded, revealing nothing more.

"We're debt free, we own this house, and we have money to travel. Hell, if we can age right, maybe we'll make it to Mars together, you and me."

"I've been unhappy here on Earth—in this house."

He glanced around the room to understand "here." Shots of their daughter at various ages smattered one cream-colored wall. Samantha's art poster of two women from the 19th century, walking down a beach with the setting sun, hung on another wall. "Unhappy. For how long?"

"A couple years. Maybe ten. Since my mother died."

His heart now raced, along with his thinking. "Ten? Why have you never mentioned this?"

"I was raised to be a 'good girl'—to serve others. I've served you and Julianne well. Now she's gone."

"I knew you were feeling some 'empty nest' thing, but—"

"I've lost myself along the way. I realize I'm taking a chance here, but I can't keep living this life."

"What life? Samantha?" He took her hand. She let him. "It's a good life. You're just depressed with Julianne leaving. We can work this out."

"I need to be me now. It's not about you. You're kind, you're generous. You've been an amazing man to live with. I love you. But you're a strong presence."

"If it's about the grocery store thing, I promise I'll call you."

"You can be self-absorbed, but it's not about that. I realize you're trying to figure out what you did wrong, but it's not about you. Can't you see?"

"I don't understand. We're stable. We love each other. How can you go from happy to 'I'm leaving you' without steps in between? We've never even argued."

"I've been a good wife, the best I can be. But I can't keep it up. I'm drowning."

That was such an odd thing to say. He realized how often she seemed to have an invisible checklist, though: Clean house, do laundry, cook, have sex.

"If you're moving from me, it's about me," he said. "Why does the love of my life want to move? This doesn't make sense."

"You have a right to be mad. I'm doing this to you, I know, but really, there are better women than me. You rushed into our marriage off of a bad one. We're very different people."

"A two-year courting and engagement is not rushing. I chose you. You're amazing, loving, sensitive, funny, slow-to-anger. In fact, I can't be angry now because I love you so much. I've been good for you. I'm not Emilio," he said, referring to her first husband, tall, physically and emotionally domineering, who openly had an affair after Samantha gave birth to Julianne. She divorced him. Two years after that, Julianne became Martin's stepdaughter.

Julianne lit a unity candle at Samantha and Martin's wedding in the Unitarian church. "We've had a good marriage for thirteen years," said Martin. "Why are you throwing this and me and our family under the bus?"

"I'm not. This may be temporary. Maybe I'll only last a week on my own—come running back with my tail between my legs. I need some solitude, a place to think."

"We have two extra rooms."

"I have to leave."

"How about we go to a marriage counselor? Will you go to a marriage counselor?"

"Yes. But I'm going to look for an apartment."

The next day, she called him from the preschool. "We have an appointment tomorrow at one p.m. with Dr. Belton, my counselor from last year. He does marriage stuff. Can you make that?"

He would tell his team they could have a late lunch, and he'd make it. "Sure," he said.

The next day, Martin arrived fifteen minutes early and sat like a lone pebble in the waiting room. Faintly, piano music, which evoked images of a lost boy, played from a lone speaker in the ceiling, wafting over a long couch, a matching chair, two end tables with lamps, and black-and-white prints of waterfalls. Ten minutes later, a man with thinning gray hair and a pot belly arrived. Martin assumed it was Dr. Belton. He carried a book entitled, *The Unfettered Mind*. "Martin?" the man said.

"Yes," and they shook hands. He seemed friendly enough.

"Samantha called and said she's running late," the doctor said, "but I can start with you."

"Okay." Martin wondered why Samantha hadn't called him. They usually called and texted each other multiple times a day. For Martin, she was his one-person network. He never thought of getting advice elsewhere.

They were like two rivers that met as one—until two days ago.

Dr. Belton ushered him into his small office, roughly eleven by eleven. It held a desk in the corner with a desktop computer, monitor, and, a tiny fountain built as a series of three rock-like pools, creating the sound of a gentle waterfall.

In the room prominently stood a cushy tall-backed chair that the Wizard of Oz might have liked, and two smaller wing chairs faced it. The doctor pointed to one of the wing chairs, where Martin sat. Martin had never spoken to a therapist alone, and he instantly felt unbalanced—or damaged, like his cherry wood desk at JPL with a gouge in the middle of it. Why was he feeling as if he had done something wrong when it was Samantha?

"So how are you feeling?" asked Dr. Belton. On the wall behind the doctor hung a wide color poster of a river that poured out of a rich green jungle into white frosty ribbons, making a gentle waterfall. More black-and-white prints of waterfalls hung on the walls. Martin felt he was falling.

He said, however, "How am I supposed to feel? Especially when your loving wife, your soulmate, tells you she's leaving when everything has been fine?"

"Clearly, it's not been fine. She'd been seeing me for depression."

"Did I cause it? Did she talk to you about me?"

"I can't betray my patient's confidentiality, but did you ever ask her what went on here?"

"Depression runs in her family."

"Let's get back to how *you* feel."

"I'm trying to understand her."

"Understanding isn't expressive of feeling. You need to give me words that denote feeling."

Martin felt like giving him a punch that denoted it.

"Are you scared, for instance?" said the doctor. "Frightened? Does the pit of your stomach feel like it's in a crashing elevator?"

"Yes, all of those."

"That's a start. How did Samantha tell you she's leaving, and how did you react?"

"We have a brown leather sofa in the living room. I was sitting there, hands on the gray remote control, when she came home. She wore her long, black dress that I love, and she announced her decision, standing above me."

"You're very visual. That tells me a lot. What did she say?"

"To tell you the truth, I feel I'm having vertigo right now." Martin held his head. The feeling quickly went away. "She said she wanted to leave, and I can't understand why. She'd been quiet a lot recently. Then two nights ago... It just didn't feel real. I mean, how can a person you love, never argue with, and enjoy want to leave? For what? I didn't sense she was troubled until after our daughter went to college."

"I see," said the doctor.

"Our daughter, Julianne, had been a pain in the butt at times in the summer, itching to be independent, missing her curfews, so by the time she left in August, I felt relieved. I could tell Samantha didn't. Never had I sensed our marriage was in trouble, though. This is just too weird."

"What were the reasons your wife gave?"

At that moment, Samantha pushed open the not-quite-closed door and entered, wearing the same black dress Martin admired from two days before. She smiled nervously. "Sorry I'm late," she said and took the seat next to Martin.

"I'm just asking Martin about the reasons you gave him for leaving," said the doctor. Samantha and the doctor looked at Martin expectantly.

"As I understand it, you need to find yourself, be a new person," Martin said to her. "Eat mashed yeast," he added, thinking of Woody Allen in *Annie Hall*.

"That's not exactly what I said," Samantha interjected. She continued talking, and many of the same words from two nights ago came back, such as "unhappy" and "good girl" and "lost." She inserted new words such as "gap," "my inner self," "lonely," and "Istanbul."

The last word made Martin realize he hadn't followed a single sentence. The scientist in him asked why couldn't he follow? Was it that he was aghast that he may have misperceived his wife all these years? He wasn't clueless. He had drunk her in.

How about if he had perceived mostly correctly? Were people really that complex—that they somehow could go "off track"? He and his team programmed for the Mars landings anything that could go wrong. They were logical. Marriage partners had logic, too, even in their chaos. If only he'd had enough information, he could have predicted this.

He saw pain in her as she spoke, but her words were still not coming through. What kind of pain kept her from talking with him earlier? That had to be the unknown factor that he did not have. Something in her past.

"So, Martin, what can you tell Samantha about all that?" asked the doctor.

"I'm thinking there's something in her past."

They looked at him as if he were the man on the street corner by Vons, babbling to himself.

"Can you put into your own words what she just said?" asked the doctor.

Could he ask her to repeat it? Instead he said, "I'm devastated. I'm lost. I don't know what you're saying," he told her.

"Let me translate for you," said the good doctor. He spoke in a soft, calm voice as the air conditioner softly whistled into the room. "She's saying she's been living a false life. She knows you don't like to argue, which your first wife did all the time, such as that blow-up you had in Istanbul, and so Samantha has met your needs but often felt angry inside."

"Why didn't she tell me?" he asked the therapist.

"Let me continue," said the doctor. "She has this huge gap between her inner and outer self. She has to move out. If she were to continue living with you, she'd have to live that false life. You don't want that, do you?"

Martin's mind whirled. "She can only be honest by moving and not seeing me? This is utterly—"

"Feeling anger is natural," said the doctor. "Soon you'll feel depressed. You're in denial now. In fact, you will go through the five stages of grief."

"What? I thought we were here to fix this thing."

"If you want to see me in sessions about your grief," said Dr. Belton, "I can make the time."

Martin glared at him, aghast. "Divorce? I go to a professional who tells me two days after hearing from Samantha that she's leaving, I have to divorce?"

"I never use the word 'divorce.'"

Samantha then spoke for a while, but Martin felt so listless and miserable, he followed nothing again. Then the doctor said, "I see our time is up. Would you like to schedule another session?"

"No," Martin barked. "I can't wrap my mind around this. This is crazy."

"I don't use the word 'crazy' either," said Dr. Belton. "Just call me when you want to see me."

But they didn't call. Rather, Samantha, inspired by the session, the next day called Martin at JPL from her preschool. "I've found an apartment in Pasadena, right in Old Town," she said. "You might find it charming. It's rather small, though. Less than five hundred square feet, including kitchen, bathroom, and closet nook."

"I thought you were waiting two months," said Martin, fingering the gouge in his desk.

"It's close to my job, close to our house. It's really best."

"Will it take pets?"

"No."

"You wanted the pets. I'm supposed to take care of all the cats?" She said nothing. He asked, "Do you have a lease?"

"It's for a year."

Martin gasped. His world was more foreign than Mars.

"It's rather expensive, so you'll have to pay our mortgage. I'll contribute what I can. I've sent you pictures," she said, rather excitedly, as if he were a girlfriend and not a husband. For her, this was an adventure. "Talk with you later," she said with a spark in her voice.

He checked his email, and there was a message from her with the subject heading "Pictures." He opened it. The first showed a square empty room with a dark wood floor, aged and scratched, thick with varnish, a small space that Van Gogh might have loved for chopping off his ear. The kitchen had a tiny stove that a munchkin might cook at. The bathroom was crammed with a tub from the Bates Motel. Why would she want something so small? Basically, it was what she could find in a day, but what was her hurry? Had he been that bad to live with?

The next morning, Samantha drove a U-Haul with a ten-foot cargo box into their driveway to move some of her stuff. She wouldn't be able to take all her things as her new place was so small. She looked happy behind the wheel, never having driven something so large before—much larger than her Mini Cooper.

"Did you get one of your friends to help?" he said, standing after she entered the dining room where he was eating Wheat Chex.

"No. My thought was to go to Home Depot and grab a day laborer."

"No way," said Martin. "Too dangerous for a woman alone. I'll help you move."

"I can't ask you."

"You don't have to. I'm doing it," he said.

She smiled. They took apart Julianne's twin bed. Julianne was in college, after all, and she could stay in the guest room with the double bed at Christmas break. Samantha's new apartment was too small for a double bed. They also carried out a bookshelf, an easy chair with an ottoman, and one narrow dresser.

At first, while Martin tried to remain good-natured about this moving and really just focus on the labor of it all, he could only think of Dr. Belton, that jerk. It was because of him Samantha was doing this. "How do you feel?" he could hear Dr. Belton say.

"I'm witnessing a reality I couldn't imagine," Martin would probably answer. No, that's not a feeling, was it? He was feeling... numb. Was numb a feeling? It was as if something in his stomach tried to pound its way out, but what would you call that? Vomit. This was vomit.

Samantha drove, and Martin let his eyes focus on nothing. The trees, houses, and cars became a mere blur as if he were in a kaleidoscope. It wasn't dark space but a world of light that seemed to mock him. Here he was, this organic creature that had little meaning compared to the age of the earth or the size of the universe. He may as well just be a single chunk of cold comet whirling between the sun and the Kuiper belt, no meaning, little purpose. He had purpose with Samantha. Now his purpose was draining like used engine oil. How was her leaving him possible?

As they drove to the new apartment, Samantha said, "This reminds me of the time we walked without a map in Venice. Remember when we found that incredible church with all that amazing art?"

He flashed on Venice, so romantic, even in the rain, all the waterways, the gardens, the flowers. She excelled at traveling most times, and he adored that about her. She'd found a cozy hotel online, a former palace with a courtyard, extremely private, down a narrow alleyway. She'd been so beautiful, naked under a mere sheet. Later, they had held hands on an arched footbridge over the water, watching gondoliers steer smiling lovers.

Caught in the moment and not censoring himself, he said, "I loved being with you there—and later in Paris looking for Jim Morrison's grave. It was like we were on the same drugs. We were as close as stripes on a barber pole."

She peered at him oddly. "What?"

He continued, "The feeling I had with you made us closer than paint on a car. I never even thought about talking about it. We just were. When we were with other people—the way you looked at me or the way you told a story that happened to us. That was our little gem."

She nodded and looked straight ahead.

As they carried the box springs up the stairs, Samantha slipped and landed on her bottom on a stair. Martin dropped his end and raced to her. "Are you all right?" he asked, helping her stand. With her face close to his, she impulsively kissed him. "Thanks for caring," she said.

He smiled. For that flash of a moment, lightning had returned.

They put her new bed together. She rolled out one of their small rugs, a white thing that fit perfectly. She'd already put up some sheer curtains. She unwrapped newspaper from around framed photographs and placed them in the bookshelf. One was a photo of him on the beach when they'd dated. She added a ceramic frog he'd bought her in Denmark. The place was looking friendly.

"I'm not going to do everything now," she said. "I just wanted you to see how quaint the place could be."

"Cute," he said.

She pulled a fluffy comforter with a flowery duvet from a box and unfurled it onto the bed.

"Very cute," he added.

She beamed and hugged him. She felt wonderfully warm, so he impulsively kissed her, and soon it became passionate. He undid her blouse, and she let him. He undid her bra, which fell to the ground. He'd always loved her breasts—she could have been a model—and at fifty-one, she still looked great. This time, she didn't shy at her nakedness. In fact, she undid the belt on his pants.

They fell on top of her comforter. She pulled down his underwear, and he pulled off her panties. While they had made love hundreds of times over the years, he didn't understand why this time felt so new, so needed, so sure. He wanted to keep going, and she seemed to want that, too.

Each time that he felt he might come, he withdrew—and then he felt he couldn't breathe. He needed to be part of her again. They tried various positions. She wasn't breathing fast, but he hoped she still felt great. He asked, "Is there something more you might like?"

"No, this is good. Keep going."

His whole soul felt catapulted into hers as if he could feel her talking to him in his head—*I am you, we are we, we are all together*. Was he hallucinating? He didn't care as his skin seemed to merge into hers. An electric field enveloped them, blue electricity as in an old mad scientist's lab. His cells twirled with hers, stardust in action. They swirled in a celestial celebration.

They kissed as they hadn't kissed in years, open mouth to open mouth, her tongue dancing with his. Connection. Selection. Celebration. The strings of the universe came into a circle.

He finally ended it, breathing hard, happy, healthy. She spooned him from behind, her hand over his heart, which beat extremely fast. They had found each other again. If her leaving brought this, every second had been worth it. She should leave every week.

They both seemed to be staring at the same photo of Julianne on her bookshelf, a shot of her at her high school graduation in a white gown, white gloves, looking confidently at the photographer, Martin.

"No matter what happens to us, she'll always be your daughter," Samantha said.

That was an odd thing for her to say, Martin thought, but he didn't want to talk about it and spoil what just happened.

As he was drifting off to sleep, Samantha whispered in his ear, "I hope you know I love you—and I always will until your new wife tells me to go away." His eyes shot open. *New wife?*

"Why did you say that last part?" he asked. "You're my wife. Why would I want anyone else? I felt so united just now. Didn't you?"

"Not really," she said, "but I know you needed it. Maybe it was a mistake, but you made me so happy today."

He couldn't sleep after that. It was a twin bed, too. He lay there on his side, still spooned, and fifteen to thirty minutes later, she sounded asleep, so he slipped out of bed. Of course, she awoke.

"Something the matter?" she asked.

"This bed isn't really meant for two," he said. "And you moved here for a reason. I shouldn't interfere."

"Thank you for understanding," she said and seemed to fall asleep again easily. He dressed, kissed her forehead, and left.

That morning, he called Dr. Belton. The man answered his own phone, and Martin said, "You remember me, Samantha's husband? You told me to divorce two days after she surprised me in wanting to leave?"

"I didn't say 'divorce'."

"What other option is there? You certainly didn't bring us back together—just the opposite. Let me offer you some feedback. You made things worse."

"I'm sorry you didn't find it helpful." The man's voice sounded as unflappable as the bankers he called when there was a wrong charge on his account.

"The next day," said Martin, "Sam took a lease on a dumpy little apartment. She shouldn't be alone the way she gets depressed. Now she is. What kind of marriage counselor are you?"

"I'm not a marriage counselor. I'm a psychiatrist. That's what the 'doctor' in front of my name is for. You didn't know that?"

"Sam said you help marriages. I mean, why else would I be there?"

"Samantha is my patient. She said she needed a safe place to meet to make you understand she's leaving. I offered that."

"And so you think I went there to be told off?"

"I'm sorry for your grief. If you'd like to see me, I can fit you in."

Martin hung up. Samantha had set him up. He wanted to talk to her about it but knew he couldn't. He didn't want to make waves. He just wanted to see her.

Weeks went by. Samantha worked so many extra shifts, she was able to contribute to the house's mortgage. "I'm worried about you," she said on the phone after she made a direct deposit to the joint account they still had. "I imposed this thing on you, so this money should help."

"I'd rather have you work less," he said, "so I could see you more." As it was, they might meet once a week for dinner or a movie. He thought they should do new things, such as zip to a Palm Springs resort or try skydiving—things they'd never done—to create new and unusual memories. He'd come to accept her new place. It was like the days of their dating. He was dating his wife, and soon she'd see that he could be sensitive and caring, more than ever. He needed her back.

"I prefer working," she said on the phone. "My contributions give me pride. It makes me feel good."

"Didn't we as a couple make you feel good?"

"Martin, dear Martin. I love you, but you're self-deluded. I wasn't a good wife for you. I'm messed up. Why don't you see?"

"We have to stay positive—because how we think makes our reality. "

"Then we have different realities. I feel bad about this, but it's better for you. How do you feel right now?"

What did he feel? he wondered. Lost. In limbo. Scared she might not come back. He could not let himself give in to this. He had to win her back. His life depended on it.

"I feel optimistic about us," he said.

"If I've learned anything since I moved in here," she said, "it's to accept uncertainty. Confusion is okay. Just *be*."

The next day, Martin had work to do in the clean room with his older colleague, Dr. Volpe. They had to wear special suits, much like astronauts. This was to avoid sending bacteria to Mars.

Volpe was a chemist and a JPL legend of a researcher who worked on how the organic compounds of life arose. He made his mark long before the first Viking craft touched down on Mars in the mid-seventies. Martin and

Dr. Volpe—Martin never called him Jerry—had to reopen part of their prototype in the clean room before it was shock tested. Whatever instrument they sent to Mars had to survive the entry, descent, and landing on the planet, which included a series of explosive bolts going off during stage separations and a parachute being deployed. Landing a rover on Mars was known as the seven minutes of terror for the twelve stages of the process, all done on autopilot.

Volpe was already in the clean room in his bunny suit when Martin danced in, feeling rather high, because while he and Samantha had not made love again since he moved her, last night they had kissed deeply outside of his car after he dropped her off from dinner. She'd been quiet at dinner, but the kiss was great.

Volpe's gray goatee and short-cropped hair shone through the clear helmet. "What's with you this morning?" said Volpe, standing at a tall desk with a part of MOXIE if front of him. "Did your wife come back?"

Martin had confided in him weeks earlier, mainly because the man seemed to know everything, and Volpe told him then, "Be confident with her. Show her your love. As the Beatles said, 'All you need is love'."

At that time, Martin had asked him how he and his wife, Trudy, always seemed so in love—holding hands at family gatherings and sometimes kissing. Did they still have sex?

"I love Trudy more than ever," said Volpe. "And, yes, the sex is good—usually on Sunday mornings. She says sometimes she looks at my fingers while we eat and thinks of how I use them. She has orgasms eighty percent of the time."

"She's seventy!" said Martin.

"Young to me," said Volpe.

Martin thought Trudy did more than accommodate. Martin's father should know.

Now Martin said, "Sam's agreed to see a new marriage counselor. I found the therapist we used years ago after Sam's mother died. It was a tough time then—not as bad as now."

"Have you and Sam had sex yet?"

Martin paused as he was about to answer, as if talking in the clean room about this were a sin. He also felt he stood in a giant condom. Martin told him of the sex when he moved her in. "The sex we had puzzles me. It was perhaps the best of my life. I felt as if in a Vulcan mind meld," he said, referring to Spock. JPLer's loved the original *Star Trek* episodes. "I couldn't get enough of her— nor she of me. We cuddled afterwards. I told her how connected I felt. She said she didn't."

Volpe shook his head.

"What?" asked Martin.

"How do you feel?"

"I don't know," said Martin. "Why do people always ask that?"

"I'd be incredibly sad—or sickened, I suppose, as if I'd been spun by too many loops in a roller coaster."

"Maybe that's what I feel."

"Do you know the research of Helen Fisher of Rutger's? She's studied the brain in love. If you had that kind of sex, you, my friend, are locked deep in romantic love, and when a person's rejected, they love harder. Your VTA is squirting dopamine all over your brain—much like cocaine causes, but in romantic love, you never come down as with cocaine."

"VTA?"

"The Ventral Tigmental Area sits right at the base of your brain in the reptilian part. What it controls is below cognitive thinking, even below your emotions. It's associated with wanting, with focus, with motivation, with craving. Romantic love—different from mere sex—is a deep addiction. I'm addicted to my wife. Look up Fisher's TED talk on YouTube."

"Where's that leave Samantha?" Martin blurted. "Why didn't she feel the same thing I did?"

"She obviously has conflicts with you. You're not the love of her life right now. Still, you have hope with another part of her brain."

"I have hope?" he said hopefully.

"Fisher says there are three parts of the brain involved in love. There's the sex part, the romantic love part, and then there's the attachment part. She still may feel deep attachment. You certainly do."

"I do. I think of her most of my day. I go back in my head, trying to figure out where it went wrong. I want her to call me or text me or email me. When she doesn't, I'm a mess. When she does, rockets could blast off. I don't feel in control. It's crazy to feel this way at sixty."

"Fisher says we can love all our lives, even if we live to ninety."

"But Sam's not loving me!"

"Listen, I feel for you. Separation is all we need to know of hell."

After they prepared MOXIE, Martin charged back to his office, reworking what he could do to win Samantha back. How hadn't he seen her pull away? Truth was he had in little ways, such as her watching what he called bludgeoning shows, true-crime stories on a true-crime channel where one spouse murdered another. One time she said, "You might push me down the stairs to make it look like an accident."

"Samantha, why do you watch those things? It's changing you."

"Don't worry. I won't murder you. I just need to unwind after work."

As he sat at his desk, again fingering its gouge, he watched a YouTube video of Helen Fisher. We were all mere biological creatures with a reptilian center in our brain squeezing out hormones: testosterone for our sex drive, dopamine and norepinephrine for hope and romance, while serotonin diminished as we became depressed over a loss. Oxytocin and vasopressin helped make us feel attached.

He didn't want to think that way. Sometimes science didn't get it. This was real for him. He needed Samantha. He'd been a fool not to show his love clearly every day of their lives. If there were a God out there, Martin promised God he'd be better, do more, until his blood moved no more through his body. He could make Samantha happy again.

He needed to tell Samantha this. She'd be at the Hummingbird Garden preschool right now. This wasn't something a phone call would do. He popped his head into Volpe's office, thanked the man, and said he was off to see Samantha.

"Good luck!" Volpe shouted.

The skies were gray. It might rain soon. The preschool operated out of a great looking home, a white Tudor mansion near Caltech, run by a pair of sisters who had fled Iran with their parents when the Shah was booted out. They had been in the Christian minority and married well in America, starting this preschool in one of their homes. It was *the* preschool for faculty at Caltech as well as the nearby upscale San Marino community, and the sisters has hired Samantha as one of two assistants. Martin walked through the courtyard, past the fountain, and rang the doorbell.

Gina, one of the sisters, opened the door and smiled broadly with her deep red lipstick. "Martin!" she said in an accent. A little girl with dark hair and ears that thrust out raced up and latched onto Gina's leg. Gina kneeled down to her height, patted her chest and said, "It's playtime in the back now. You know that. Skedaddle." The little girl took off.

"Is Samantha available?"

"Sure. You want to come in?"

"I just need to talk with her privately a moment."

"I'll get her," said Gina.

Soon Samantha stood at the door and appeared surprised. *Surprised happy or surprised shocked?* Martin asked himself. He hoped for the former.

"Wow," said Samantha. "I don't think you've come here in a couple of years. What's up?"

"Has it been that long?" asked Martin, feeling that was a clue, too. He would have to come more often. "Can we talk out here?"

She nodded, stepped out, and they moved closer to the fountain, one bowl spilling into the next. Samantha said, "I'm going to see you this weekend. It couldn't wait?" Arms folded, she looked impatient.

"I have a few possible times with the marriage counselor," Martin said. "I wanted to check with you."

"That only needs a phone call."

"I miss you," said Martin. "I don't know what's going on with me. I'm not used to these... feelings."

"You know I care for you. You'll always be my friend."

"Friends I have. Soulmates—you're the only one."

"If I don't come back, you'll find someone new within six months, trust me. You're a handsome guy."

"I'm sixty! Who wants some guy with high cholesterol, whose internal organs are about to disintegrate?"

"You're exaggerating."

"I'm serious," he said. "Time has meaning when I'm with you. I feel meaningless without you."

"Your Mars mission has much more importance than me or what I do."

He shook his head violently and looked away. The sky over one mountain had a clear spot. He said, "I can have knowledge and still be dumb."

The curtains in the nearest window moved. The little girl from before and two little boys with short hair stared at them curiously. Martin pointed to them. "Life is here on Earth," he said to Samantha. "You're helping build the leaders of tomorrow."

Samantha turned, saw the faces, laughed and made shooing motions. The kids giggled and ran off.

"Besides," said Martin, "I love your jokes, your music, your sexy new pants," he said as he placed his hands on her hips. He knelt before her. "Marry me, Samantha. Marry me again."

"We're still married. What are you talking about?"

"We'll find the minister who married us, and we'll have friends over, tell them it's a barbecue, and we'll renew our vows. I don't think you see how much I love you, think of you, obsess over you. You're my everything. My pack of gum. My lip balm. My tweezers. Life, Mars, manned missions are meaningless without you."

Rather than give him some quip as he expected, Samantha jerked in a spasm. She was crying. Martin stood and held her close. She let him.

"Are you okay?" he asked.

"No, I'm not okay," she said. "Every fiber in my body wants to come back to you. But that's what I've done my whole life—do what others want of me. I was the good girl as a teenager, did what my parents told me, went to the community college they arranged. I married the first guy they liked for me, and he was a controlling asshole."

"I'm not. Second marriages are good."

"I'm messed up. I want to be messed up on my own."

"I can help. Let's be messed up together."

"I can't be a wife anymore." She wiped at her tears. "I can't be in a role. I just want to be me."

He sighed. How to make her see? He just needed the right words. He said, "We'll be a force against the world. The world is a harsh place, and look at our marriage. We did well. We have a great house, great pets. We don't have debt. We don't argue. We love our jobs. We—"

"And if I move back with you, in that jail of a house, my life will be over."

"Why would you say that?"

"You've been a great dad to Julianne. A very good dad. She'll still be your daughter."

"You keep saying that as if—" And then it struck him. Samantha had married him to be a father, not a lover. She'd pretended all those years to be in love with him, to adore him, to advise him, to cuddle him, to play the role of wife, but this marriage was really about Julianne. That was the deal.

Had he really been that much of a fool? "I see," he said, barely getting the words out. "Julianne. You... You..."

"What?"

"Hallowed be thy name."

"What?"

"Your mother once said she'd been worried about you being a single mom. Now I get it."

"No. I've loved you."

"Julianne goes off to college, and now you're gone. I get it."

"No! Love is like milk. There's an expiration date. Our milk has gone sour."

"Our milk can be renewed."

She looked down, shaking her head.

He turned to the side, again seeing the little faces of a new generation. Their innocent faces pushed him to say, "And what will your life be without me? Divided, we'll have much less—emotionally, financially, and even ergonomically because we fit together like shoes. Do you want to be lonely shoes?"

"I'm sorry, Martin. You'll be happy. You'll see. Yes, I'll probably be alone, but I won't be making anyone miserable. Look at how miserable you are."

"Because I'm not with you!"

She paused. "Forget the marriage counselor. We're over. I'm sorry," and she hurried back into the house. Gina happened to stand just inside the doorway, peering at him as if to say what the hell had he done to Samantha?

With a clap of thunder, the rain started. Soon it came down in a wind that drove the rain sideways, right into Martin's face and eyes. He sat in his car, his Mini Cooper, and went over in his mind what just happened. What if he'd said he chose her because she was so true-to-heart, so honest, so true to her emotions that she'd always been his extra eyes. She had an extra sense that he didn't have, much like a bloodhound could smell danger.

He drove in the rain for an hour, mostly on freeways, until he witnessed a car just ahead of him spin crazily and smash into the concrete barrier that separated them from oncoming traffic. He passed the damaged car, an older woman at the wheel, now stopped in the fast lane, and Martin quickly maneuvered to the slow lane to call 911. Once on the shoulder, though, he looked back. Red emergency lights twirled, and a police car had stopped right behind the wreck. The woman would be all right. Martin asked himself why was he putting himself in peril by driving in the rain? Southern California drivers didn't understand the physics of rain, and they drove the same fast speed as on a sunny day. Physics was everything.

Shaken, he pulled off the freeway. Soon he crawled the streets of Pasadena, Old Town, in fact. Samantha's apartment was close. She'd probably be home by now. Should he knock on her door and ask forgiveness? Yes, he told himself. He could still make this better.

He found his big black umbrella in his trunk and started walking in the downpour, but the closer he got, the stupider he felt, all this while his heart clenched. Everything about what he was doing said *wrong*. He needed to sit down. In Old Town, every place was quaint. Across the street, not far from Sam's apartment, a set of green awnings hung over a set of huge picture windows, displaying the words "Coffee. Tea. Life." He needed life.

He dashed across the street. As he headed toward the place, he saw a thin man at a circular table by a window, and the man looked, oddly, much like himself at that age, late twenties with longish hair and a dark leather jacket. The fellow cut into a scoop of vanilla ice cream in a paper bowl and raised his spoon to a young woman with sensuous lips. He fed her the vanilla. Her lips pulled off the spoon, making it clean.

Martin stood there like an icicle for many seconds more, holding his umbrella up, even though it wasn't needed under the awning. He tried to catch his breath. It was as if the air wasn't air anymore.

The young couple turned, saw him, and frowned. He quickly ran, still struggling for air. His red-and-black car stood just ahead, and he dove in. After starting the car, he took off. The universe screamed at him as he did so.

The next morning, the radio came on at six a.m. as usual. Stock market futures were up. Gold futures were up. On his bed, all five cats were curled up next to him, two on each side and one at his feet, like stays to a tent keeping him in place. The black-and-white cat purred. Martin didn't move anything except his hands across the nearest pets. He had to get going. Today they'd shock test MOXIE.

He ate two English muffins—high in sodium, smothered with salted butter.

At JPL, MOXIE looked like an Erector-set creation—mostly a metal box with supports on the sides. It stood in the testing room atop a white polished column that would deliver the simulated shocks of explosive bolts and jerks associated with a Mars entry and landing. On either side, two halves of a giant red vise gripped the column.

Various black wires fed into MOXIE, and the wires led off to various meters. A monitor showed three graphs, looking like an EKG screen at a hospital. Four men, including Martin, and three women stood in the room. Half of the group were old-timers like Dr. Volpe, people brought out of retirement to work on the project. The others had a lot of experience, too. These people would make it possible for men and women to live on Mars. Martin wondered if any Mars colonists would fall in and out of love, only to be severely depressed on the red planet.

Dr. Volpe said something about potatoes, referencing the movie *The Martian,* and everyone laughed except Martin. He wondered at that moment what Samantha was doing. Maybe she'd be taking her break right now and ordering French fries.

The first explosive shock happened sooner than Martin expected, and he leapt to his left. No others in the room noticed. The pain in his chest and one arm became incredibly intense. He fell to the ground just as the second explosive simulation occurred, and people in the room, looking at the flat screen, purred.

Martin gasped for air, wondering what was happening. Ever so briefly he thought, "Was this it?" He should have realized it was a heart attack, but rather, a sense of calm overcame him just as the pain left him. Soon, he didn't care, leaping over the stages of grief—denial, anger, bargaining, and depression—right to acceptance, even as a deep bass chord played in his mind.

His eyes now closed, he didn't notice himself on the ground. He didn't hear someone say, "This is going to work." He didn't think about the half-and-half he left out on the counter at home, his home, Samantha's home. He didn't think about how houses outlasted people, and somewhere in his house's future, a new couple would live.

He didn't wonder who would feed the cats tonight. Rather, he thought of Mars, his red planet, and, laughing, thought he should have studied Venus. Perhaps that would that have helped him understand love and Samantha.

As his heart slowed toward a stop, he smelled white jasmine, the flowers at his home, outside his bedroom. He thought of the very first night Samantha slept in his bed, his fingers against her fingers, their hands the same size. After they made love for over a half hour, they took a break for a midnight snack, Oreo cookies and cantaloupe, chocolate and fruit just perfect, and they made love again. He hadn't slept right away but rather listened to her breathe. In the dark, it was a soft sound, almost like a cat purring, ending with the swish he imagined of an arrow sliding into snow. Her breathing. Purr, swish. Purr, swish. This unique and wonderful human being next to him. There was no better deal.

A Dog Story

Today, Chelsea would get the dog, which she had left with her soon-to-be-ex-husband. She was the one to choose the dog, but she had to leave poor Scrappy behind—complicated, just too complicated.

Chelsea would have her work cut out for her today as she still had to clean her West Valley studio apartment. Scrappy liked a clean kitchen.

She was still in bed. Dan always used to get her her morning coffee. That remained a big downside of moving out.

Dan had offered Scrappy for Mother's Day. He insisted Scrappy was his dog now, but he was happy to let her have him for a day or two. Dan would feed and walk Scrappy and leave him in the house for her because he was going to Palm Springs. She still had a key to the house.

Two hours later and in front of the house, Chelsea rummaged in her big leather bag for her keys. She worried she might chip her freshly painted red nails. The nail salon had been a treat for herself. Small things helped.

They're here, they're here, she thought of the keys. She just wanted to grab the dog and get away. This house gave her weird vibes. As she felt the keychain and pulled it from her purse, the front door swung open, startling her, and her keychain fell onto the Italian tile, sending out a jingling sound as if from Santa Claus.

"Ah, you're here," said Dan, looking surprisingly upbeat for having been dumped by her six months earlier. He had tried to woo her back, but it didn't work. A month ago, she had cancelled the marriage counselor and asked for a divorce. His long gray hair had a new cut, and he was in the blue terrycloth robe she'd bought him for his last birthday. He looked good.

"I didn't expect—" she said. "Not in Palm Springs?"

"Cancelled," he said.

"So you don't need me to—"

"Take the dog for Mother's Day. He loves you."

"Hardly." She didn't go any further.

"How's work?" he asked, as if to keep the conversation going.

"I'm editing a book about World War Two—like we need another book on the subject."

"Everyone loves Churchill," he said. "Will Hope be back today and take you out to dinner?" he said, referring to their daughter.

"Hope won't be here," Chelsea said. "Mother's Day isn't high on her list." Hope was returning from Cal State Stanislaus in Turlock, where she was studying to be a veterinarian. Her going to college was when their problems all started. Chelsea felt empty. Empty nest, empty life.

"What's she doing instead?" he asked.

"Camping."

"Alone?"

"She didn't say."

"I wonder if she's in love," he said. "Good ol' love.... Did you tell her about our decision to actually divorce?"

"No. She was going into finals. I didn't want to distract her."

He paused. She knew he was trying hard not to be critical. Of course, she should have told Hope, but Hope wasn't speaking to either of them. Hope only sent them short texts. "And where's she going to stay on her return?" he asked.

"Here, I assume." Chelsea had her apartment off Topanga Boulevard in the flats—a small studio with only a twin bed and a sofa—a love seat, actually. No room for Hope. The place was ridiculously expensive, and Chelsea wasn't supposed to have pets. She'd sneak Scrappy in. If only there were a way for Chelsea to sneak back into Hope's heart.

"She's still not taking my calls, blaming me for this," he said.

"It's not much better for me."

He opened the door wider and ushered her in. On the other side, their dog, Scrappy, a mixed breed, mostly terrier, stared at Chelsea as if she were the humane society at the door to give him the needle.

"It's okay, Scrappy," said Chelsea, but the dog backed up.

"This is your mommy," said Dan with enthusiasm, and the dog's tail wagged quickly, with Scrappy looking up lovingly at him. Poor Scrappy didn't know how cold Dan could be.

"He's a good dog," said Dan.

After Hope had turned seven, Chelsea found Scrappy at the local pound amid the Pit Bulls and Pinschers, German Shepherds and bullmastiffs. In a cage meant for attack dogs stood a tiny terrier-esque dog who could have been bred at Chernobyl, brown wiry hair askew with a blond streak at his crown as if painted there by a pixie. Hope had named him Scrappy, although for a while, under his breath, Dan came to call him Crappy. Still, for his daughter, he pretended to love the little dog. In time, he did, and sometimes he now called him "Cap" for "Captain." Hope was eighteen, off to college, and ready to be a vet, thanks to Scrappy. Now here Chelsea stood like a stranger in her former Woodland Hills home.

"Scrappy'll be fine," Dan reassured her. "He has special powers."

She could only sigh. Scrappy had fixed nothing in their marriage. Chelsea had often felt lonely before she fled. An affair before she left, with a neighbor who she ran into at the dog park, helped her realize sex could be better than with Dan, who was always too quick. He often complained he could see pain on her face. She told him it was her body. "I'm fifty. That's old for a woman," she had said.

"You're beautiful, absolutely beautiful," he'd replied. Truth was, she didn't know why she felt so pained with Dan—maybe because for him sex was expected. She'd become his shadow. Hell, she didn't know what she wanted anymore except out. She'd found her apartment in a day.

"Would you like some coffee?" Dan asked, and she moved into the kitchen with him before saying "No thanks." Her eyes went to the rearranged glass cupboards. They weren't so crowded anymore.

As if hearing her thoughts, he pointed to a box on the counter. "I thought you'd want your mother's china back, so I wrapped each piece in newspaper the way you taught me."

"Oh. Thank you," she said. "I'd been meaning to do that."

"You need to know I never took you for granted," said Dan. "You just had a need for privacy, so I left you alone."

"The marriage falling apart wasn't just me."

"I know," he said, nodding. "I wasn't good at asking questions, right?"

"Is that a question?"

She knew he didn't understand her quietness—maybe because he was so outgoing. How could she trust him when he was so normal?

"It's about communication," their counselor, Tracy, had said. "Even a simple touch can communicate a lot."

Dan stared at her. She could get so caught up in her thoughts. "Sorry," she said. "Scrappy and I will go."

"He'll be good for you." Dan petted the dog. "Good, Cap. Help your mommy."

As she connected Scrappy's leash, Chelsea noticed on the counter Dan's file folder, marked "Mark Taper Forum." It's where he kept their subscription theatre tickets.

"Is the next play today?" she asked.

"Yes," he said. Scrappy looked at her as if shaking his head. Then she asked Dan, "Did you find someone to go with you?"

"Uh huh."

"Oh, who?"

"Funny where life takes its turns. I ran into Birdie at Starbucks last month."

Her heart jolted. "My once-best-friend and maid of honor?" Birdie was a tall buxom Argentinian.

"I never understood why you lost touch with her."

Because she made me feel I wasn't good enough, she thought but said nothing.

"She's very nice."

"She's your girlfriend now?"

He smiled sheepishly and shrugged. "She tells me how she feels. That's refreshing."

Covering, she turned for the door, pulling Scrappy, saying, "Oh, that's nice."

But why hadn't Hope told her? Why hadn't Birdie said anything?

"You asked," he said. "I'm not trying—"

"No, no, that's fine," Chelsea told Dan. "She's single, you're soon-to-be single." Scrappy sat. She tugged more and opened the front door. "I just didn't expect Birdie." General George Patton taking Messina in World War Two surprised everyone, too.

"Chelsea, those first three months after you left, you had to see I was devastated. I was dying. I'd wake up thinking, 'Fuck, another day?' My life was over. You were the love of my life and— I mean, what was real anymore?"

"You're exaggerating."

Scrappy followed Chelsea onto the tile outside as if now accepting his mission.

"Those poems I wrote you," he said. "The texts, the dinner dates with you, didn't you see—"

"It felt like a campaign," she said. "It was too much."

"I loved you," said Dan. "But I finally understood. You didn't want me."

Scrappy looked at Dan, then Chelsea, then back again, tilting his head as if not understanding.

"I didn't want to give you pain," she said.

"It's taken me six months. My life has to go on. I just can't wait and—"

"No, that's fine. I didn't mean to...." She didn't know what she meant. She'd felt ignored by him when married, and after she left, his tsunami of constant interest swept in. She was confused.

"I told you two months ago I might date," he said. "You could have stopped me. You could have come back."

"No, really, I'm sorry," but the pounding in her head kept pulsing with the words, *stupid girl, stupid girl.* Scrappy looked at her and gave a low growl. She hurried off the porch toward her car, a blue Prius, hurrying the dog along.

"It's not necessarily serious," he said. "Maybe I'm not ready."

"You're a handsome guy," she said without facing him. "Just listen to Birdie. Don't go on with your monologues."

"That was always me nervous. When you became quiet, I just thought...." He didn't go on. It was all stuff from marriage counseling. They were two nice people who didn't like to confront conflict. Now here they were—and he was going on to a life, perhaps, with Birdie, leaving Chelsea behind. Birdie had seen a good thing. She'd always admired Dan. The pairing was as natural as Rommel driving deep into Egypt. Fuck. Chelsea knew she deserved this heartbreak, but now the universe was also screaming at her.

She hurried to her back door. Scrappy jumped in. She kept it open for Dan, who was just behind with the box of dishes. She jumped into the front seat so he wouldn't see her face. As he leaned in to gently place the box on the back seat, she started the car.

"Thank you. Bye."

He shut the rear door. "Bye," he said, muffled through the window.

She zoomed through their walled community, *stupid girl, stupid girl,* and Scrappy squeaked, staring at her.

"What?" she said to Scrappy. "I'm driving fine." When the front gate to the community rolled aside to the left for her, she pushed ahead too quickly and moved too close to the metal post on the right side. The post raked the far side of the car with a sound like a submarine being crushed by the depths. Fuck!

She pulled over and looked at the damage to the rear door. Paint on the side had been scraped to the bare metal. The whole car probably needed to be painted, a couple thousand dollars. It was all she could do to pay for her apartment and half the mortgage. She insisted on paying her half still.

Before she got back in the car, she texted Birdie. "I just saw Dan. He said you two are dating. Were you going to tell me?" Nothing returned from Birdie. Chelsea shoved the phone back into her rear pocket and returned to the driver's seat.

She thought of Churchill's quote, *If you are going through hell, keep going.* She kept going. At the first light, she heard a car honk loudly; tires screeched, and her car got punched to the side with the sound of dishes shattering. Scrappy flew against the passenger door. The light had been green, hadn't it? She couldn't remember, now that she had hit her head against the driver's side window. Scrappy barked at her, angry—barked and barked.

"You okay?" She cuddled him. Soon he stopped wrestling.

A loud knocking came on her window. "Lady, what were you thinking?" A man about Dan's age in a polo shirt and a Dodger baseball cap looked shaken.

"It's not my fault," she said. "Sometimes two people can be—"

"You did this! It's your doing."

"I mean, it may *look* like that, but—" She undid her seatbelt. "I'm not clear how. It just happened."

"You blasted through a red light!"

She stepped out with Scrappy on his leash, and the dog was quiet now. The man's Suburban had bashed her car in the rear door that she had scraped. The Suburban looked fine. Scrappy seemed fine. Everything was fine except her, her car, and her marriage.

The police came, but she refused an ambulance. She just wanted her dog to be okay, and Scrappy sat on the ground patiently. She would not call Dan. The car still drove.

Finally at her apartment, and after seeing three of her painted nails were chipped, she prepared dinner. Scrappy gobbled high-end dog food of chicken and sweet potato. She'd microwaved a burrito for herself because the stove didn't work in her apartment, and she'd never told the manager. She just didn't want people in her life right now.

After dinner, she led Scrappy outside to do his business. She'd forgotten he was anal retentive. Dan almost always walked the dog, so she rarely had to watch Scrappy sniff different bushes, trees, flowers, lampposts, rocks, and gravel areas, looking for the perfect spot. He'd pee occasionally, making his "Scrappy was here" spots, but he wouldn't poop. "Come on, Scrappy, you're wearing me out," she said four blocks down. The dog kept looking back at her as if judging her, which creeped her out. "What? I'm fine," she said. Finally she stopped him. "Where are you going? Can't you just do your stuff?"

But the dog kept walking as if he knew his destination.

"You've never been here," she told the dog. "Warner Park's too far. You can't possibly know about it." Still, the dog kept walking determinedly and looking occasionally back at her until they arrived at Warner Park. He spun three times in a spot near a trash bin and pooped. She cleaned up after him.

By the time they returned, she felt better. The walk had put her in a better mood—until her phone dinged to announce a text message. Scrappy barked as she pulled out her cell phone from her back pocket. Then he started to paw the door.

"Behave!" she told him. "I don't want to be kicked out of here." She read the message—from Birdie: "I wanted Dan to bring it up. You and I never talk anymore, anyway—sorry, buddy. I thought you wouldn't care."

"Ah!" she screamed. She couldn't help herself. Then she heard someone in the hallway say loudly, "I heard a scream."

She covered her mouth and plopped onto her love seat. Scrappy pawed harder and barked louder as if he needed another walk. The manager would probably soon be banging on her door, and she'd be thrown out, or so she imagined, and she fell sideways onto the love seat like a statue in a museum after a tank attack. Her husband was dating. Her daughter didn't talk with her—and now a dog, a fucking little dog, was upset with her. She couldn't even make a dog happy. Chelsea pounded her head against the cushion, back and forth, back and forth, but when she punched her feet out, she hit the floor lamp, which crashed to the ground with the light bulb exploding.

On the worst Mother's Day ever, Chelsea squeezed her head, not wanting to cry as she felt her eyes pooling. A dog jumped onto her lap and then jabbed his feet into her chest. His tongue slid across her cheek—a simple, beautiful touch.

She opened her eyes. With his mouth open, tongue out, Scrappy gleamed. Winston Churchill, stoic, irascible Churchill, was a softie for his dogs, too. "I love you, my beast." She kissed Scrappy on the head. He seemed to nod.

I'd Rather Die than Go to North Dakota

W hen Ayako awoke that morning next to her husband, Finn, in their cramped Hollywood apartment and saw the red splatter on his T-shirt, she was reminded of the spaghetti sauce she'd thrown against him and the wall the previous evening. He'd asked if she would mind if he went alone to a movie. This was after he explained that he'd accepted a job as a video editor in Fargo, North Dakota. At the stove, she dipped a scoop and flung it.

She looked at Finn's form in bed. He looked like a tuna roll. Rather than wake him, she moved to the window. The sun was just rising, and she wanted to create a poem in her head.

> *The satellite dish*
> *Blocks the rising silent sun*
> *And stares into the void.*

Poems relaxed her. So did thinking of herself as a poet—better than seeing herself as a waitress. She had trained in Tokyo to teach poetry, and now this. But wasn't this a hell of a lot better than her first husband, who had abandoned Kelly and her in Kentucky? Ayako and Kelly had then moved farther west to Los Angeles, where there were more Japanese people, and Ayako found a waitressing job at a Japanese restaurant, Asahi Ramen. There, she'd met Finn—as different as anyone she'd known. He was who she'd wanted. But North Dakota?

She was putting on her bra when she heard, "You're beautiful." Finn was grinning. "All your swimming looks good on you."

"I know what you're doing."

"What?"

"Being nice."

"Isn't that what life's about?"

"I don't know what it is."

"It's a new day," he said in his cheery voice. "Let's enjoy it."

That was enough of that. In just her bra and panties, she pushed into the bathroom where she could be alone for at least a few minutes. She wasn't sure she could take his optimism right now.

On the toilet, she realized Finn perhaps didn't understand her needs. Americans liked to talk. She should talk—better than flinging sauce. She flushed, washed her hands, and returned to the bedroom.

"I like Los Angeles," she announced.

"You hate it. You always complain."

"That's called venting."

He laughed. "I taught you that word. So you believe it? You're venting?"

"Why can't we stay here?"

"Because we need money. Because the cost of living here is too high. Because you said if I found a great job anywhere, you'd move."

She clenched her teeth. She had said that. She just didn't think there were such jobs outside of Los Angeles. "How about if you look for another job for another week?"

"That would mean saying no to Prairie Public Broadcasting, which is great money. And it's cheap to live in North Dakota."

"What if I said I'd rather die than go to North Dakota?"

"You know you don't mean that." He patted the bed. "Come here. Let's snuggle and talk about this."

She knew what that meant. They'd hold each other, then his gentle hands would undo her bra, and then, well. "Okay," she said. "But no talking." She could use a little loving.

After they made love—make-up sex was always the best—they cuddled, with Finn behind her and his long arm with his delicate fingers curled against her.

> *A warm cave of flesh*
> *Cups my backside and Finn purrs*
> *That Dakota rocks.*

She spoke. "I'm sorry about last night. I am sorry about my anger. I will do better."

"So we can go to North Dakota?"

"I didn't say that."

"Will you think about it?"

"Sure."

"Fit in another swim today. It always relaxes you."

Maybe it would. She didn't need him telling her so. "North Dakota? I still don't know where it is." She hadn't taken her citizenship test yet, so she didn't know the fifty states.

"In the middle of America toward the top, near Minnesota. You saw that hilarious movie, *Fargo*."

"Isn't North Dakota flat and cold?"

"Not in the summer—then it's warm and hilly."

"And what am I supposed to do there?"

"They have restaurants. They need waitresses."

"Asian?" she said, hearing her own strong accent.

"Sure. Or you can learn to be an accountant. That's what you want, right?"

"I want to teach poetry."

"That's not realistic. Americans don't understand poems. They don't want their kids to understand them, either."

"Haiku is easy to get—same with tanka and death poems."

"Death poems? No way. Americans don't like death. In fact, Congress is going to pass a bill to get rid of death."

She smiled. "Okay, so I will learn numbers." Accounting was stable. Moving to a place that no one had heard of wasn't. Then again, until she moved to Kentucky, she hadn't known much about that state, either, beyond the Toyota plant and Kentucky Fried Chicken. "What about Kelly?" she said.

"They have first grade there. She can start in the fall. Kids adapt."

Kelly was her six-year-old daughter from her previous marriage. She'd left Japan with Shuichi, a respected physicist, when he had landed a major job at the University of Kentucky. They had to move across the world. She'd had to learn English and a whole new life. Soon he wanted sex doggie style. Everything was strange. He'd then fallen in love with a redheaded coed named Kelly—this was after they had named their own daughter Kelly at his suggestion—and he left them. Now would there be pretty young women at Prairie Public Broadcasting?

Later, as Ayako drove Kelly to school, Ayako glanced at her daughter in the mirror. She was short but looked tall in the back seat in her red-and-blue uniform.

"Finn says I can have a dog in North Dakota," Kelly said.

"He's bribing you."

"That's okay. I want a terrier."

"Why can't I get what I want?" Ayako said.

"What do you want?"

"Tums." Her stomach gurgled; she needed the confusion to stop.

After she'd dropped Kelly off at the private school in the Valley, she found herself sitting in her car on the street for nearly an hour, watching parrots gather in a large eucalyptus tree, screeching their horrible squawks. Both things, parrots and eucalyptus, were not native to the area. They'd seemed to adapt. She kept thinking, however, how she'd convinced her brother to come over from Japan. He died in a freak accident at a warehouse in Kentucky. His wife then died in a car accident on the way home from the funeral. Their blood was on her hands.

At noon, Ayako wheeled her shopping cart around Vons and came to the yogurt section. She faced colors in funny-shaped containers—enough to hammer the insensate into feeling. She felt a tingle.

> *Some say that Yoplait*
> *is healthy, but if you don't*
> *care, then what is it?*

She avoided the curdled milk products and picked up instead a packet of Bays English muffins. It was one way to absorb more English. She also liked the word "muffins."

> *I'd like to stuff him*
> *Full of muffins and make him*
> *Be a waiter once.*

She plopped the Bays into the basket. When she'd met Finn, he said he loved everything Japanese. He got along so well with Kelly, too, that after a few months, they moved in together. One household was cheaper than two. True, Ayako had urged Finn to look for better jobs. Working freelance on one low-budget movie or another didn't make it, not after they'd married and were a family. Why was he always so sure of things?

In the afternoon, before she slipped into her Speedo and dashed to the lap pool, Ayako found the atlas. North Dakota appeared rectangular. Minnesota, on the other hand, looked like a teakettle with a spout and knob top. Why couldn't they move there?

She found herself crying. It was as if two giant hands squeezed her. No amount of green tea would help. Only swimming might comfort. The pool drew her like the promise of starlight. The one great thing about their apartment was the pool.

Outside, the sun, like a former husband, gave her no warmth. She found herself shivering, even though the air was quite warm. No one was there. She stared at the sign: "No Lifeguard on Duty. Absolutely No Diving."

She must take control. Finn could do things. So could she. She moved by the stairs and dropped her towel. She would run and dive, and compose the best poem of the day. She stared at the blue water and the concrete between her and the pool. The pool was edged with tan tile that had a lip.

> *My first step is short*
> *But firm. I run more surely*
> *Now, fast and feeling*

Feeling what? She had more words. The poem must go longer. After all, there are longer poems.

Free, but I must go faster.

Yes, true.

The edge is oily and—

She felt herself slip. Her feet jutted out from her. The hard edge beckoned. Her head would surely crash. She had one more syllable:

Oh!

The Benefits of Breathing

R ay woke up smiling, which, these days, his wife thought unreasonable. After all, he'd been declining. He might feel lightheaded standing up from the couch, fall, and Julie his wife would come running in with her short gray hair flying. He'd say, "No broken bones."

"I don't understand why," she said one night. "Don't you think it's time for a cane?"

"I'm a Midwesterner—strong bones from milk—and I don't feel old."

This morning, still partly in a dream, Ray was golfing at St. Andrews in Scotland, his ball flying high over the rippled fairway and the golf course that had started golf. He'd been with a client, Gordon Marx, whom he hadn't seen or thought of in years, and they gazed at the northerly bay, sea grass near the shore. Ray had been a successful stockbroker in San Francisco, head of the international department, but it was partly because he loved doing things with his clients, such as golfing in Scotland or attending an opera in Italy. He loved people.

His dreams, lately, brought him an array of minor characters from his life – not his parents, not his three wives, not his three daughters (one from each marriage) – but he saw such people as his golfer friend John, the grumpy grocery lady from his childhood in Vancouver, and the kid Mike, who'd wiped his bloody finger on his gym T-shirt in P.E. in eighth grade. Add in the bearded Viet vet he'd once given five dollars to at a stop sign in San Francisco.

As Ray blinked awake with a black cat on one side of him, a Siamese cat on the other, he could only shake his head, wondering why his dreams lately couldn't be more entertaining. He understood he was dying, but why was it taking so long? Months. Couldn't the end be more interesting?

Ray reflected on St. Andrews. He'd beaten Gordon by eight strokes. These days, his game of golf, which had held up until just before age ninety, had evaporated completely. As he thought about it, his ninetieth birthday at the nearby Villa Restaurant might have been his last great day. From the hilltop eatery, he had soaked in the beautiful spring-green mountains of Santa Rosa, not a house or structure in sight.

His oldest child, Kathleen, then sixty-five, her back to him, sun in her hair, stared at a turkey vulture gliding high on the thermals. The bird of prey undoubtedly scanned for something dying. Kathleen turned back to the table, and, stepping forward in three swinging steps, her arms moving with a little Cuban action, made a cha-cha-cha.

"You've always been a good dancer," said Ray. She'd once taught him the four basic steps to the dance, the first being to step forward-forward-forward.

At the table, Kathleen raised her champagne glass high. "To you, Dad."

"To Ray, light of my life," said Julie in a stunning green dress, also raising her flute. Ray noticed them both reflected in the glass he raised.

"To you two," he said. "You've made my life especially worthwhile."

"I thought I drove you crazy," said Julie.

"I have lived with sweet you for forty years," he said, clinking her glass. "Forty-one may be a challenge."

He turned to Kathleen, raising his glass once again. "And to you and your siblings."

"You know Erica's at a conference in Italy, and Suzanne's father-in-law—"

"Listen, I begrudge nothing. I'm happy you're here."

"Better than mud-luscious Minnesota."

In the nine months since that birthday, Ray had fallen, lightheaded, at least half a dozen times while standing or walking, and twice he'd tripped over one of his wife's five cats. He hadn't broken anything, but the falls beat up his face badly. Still, he smiled. What's the alternative, right?

These days, he wheeled himself around the house in a type of wheelchair where he pushed with his legs. Old age was like sausages left out in the sun too long, bloating, ready to burst. That's also how his ankles now appeared. He couldn't wear shoes anymore. Still, it wasn't painful. The end just seemed to be like an awkward stageplay where the playwright forgot why he wrote it in the first place. He figured, though, that Samuel Beckett knew what he was doing even if most people thought *Waiting for Godot* was pointless. Life was absurd, but you had to laugh anyway.

Old age also brought him breathlessness, a lack of concentration, and a loss of hearing so that his conversations with Julie, younger than he by twenty years, rarely went beyond four sentences, such as now, when he got out of the bathroom.

Ray: (*yelling from the bedroom*) Where are my shorts? (*She yells something back that he does not understand.*) WHAT?

Julie: (*louder*) What are you selling short? I thought you weren't trading anymore.

Ray: My shorts! My favorite gray shorts.

Julie: You peed in them yesterday. I haven't done the wash yet.

Ray: I'm going back to sleep.

He did sleep after he pulled on pants, as laborious an exercise as a half-hour in the gym used to be. He also could be disoriented. One time, waking up in his wheel-chair, he was sure he was in a trailer, locked-in and abandoned. It was his home office, but he had recognized nothing.

The doorbell rang, and Julie shouted out, "I'll get it! I'm sure it's Suzanne!"

Suzanne? he thought. Why was she here from Wyoming? He shook his head a few times to return to the world. He wheeled himself into the living room.

"Hi, Dad," said Suzanne, blond-haired and waving from the front door. Her smile seemed forced, which wasn't like her. His youngest child had become a broker in his footsteps. She lived in Jackson, Wyoming, where there were three ski resorts and a tall, skinny husband who loved to ski with her. Working at an independent wealth management company, Suzanne and her chef husband Frankie had never had children. Two of Kathleen's often flew to Wyoming to ski with Aunt Suzanne and Uncle Frankie. Ray had four other grandchildren, and two great-grandchildren.

To Suzanne he said, "What're you doing here? I'm not dead yet."

"Can you hear me?" she said.

With one of his blasted hearing-aids missing, he could not hear her clearly, but he made out her words and said, "Yes, I can hear you."

Julie swooped into the room with a lemonade and a hug for Suzanne. The two women briefly peered at each other guiltily, and then Julie pulled Suzanne into the kitchen. Ray could make out Suzanne's words, "Are you sure?" and he heard part of Julie's reply, "He's still a parent and a human being."

"What's going on?" he demanded.

"Thanks, Julie," said Suzanne. "I'll take Dad out to the sunporch." She grabbed the handles and guided him across the living room to the former screened porch, now enclosed and air conditioned.

Suzanne stopped right at a picture window, which overlooked his ten-acre hillside vineyard. Affixed to wires and drip irrigation, the vines in straight rows glistened heavy with fruit, there at the end of the summer. Within weeks, St. Francis Winery would send workers to pick the fruit once it had attained a certain sweetness. He had worked daily on his vines up to age ninety.

Suzanne crouched beside him and looked into his eyes. "Dad. I have something to tell you." The room was free from distracting noises, so he could hear her better.

"I can guess," he said. "You love me, and you'll miss me. You didn't have to fly here for that."

"Yes, that's all true. I love you."

"Circle of life, right?" he said. "It feels like a damn wall, right now, but I'm looking for the secret tunnel under it."

"There's something else," Suzanne said, her eyes glistening, watery, even if her face remained calm. She'd always been stoic.

"What is it, honey? Divorce?"

She frowned. "No," she said. "Why would you say that? Jimmy and I hang-glide together."

"You hang-glide?" he said, worry in his voice.

"It's a metaphor, Dad."

"Ah. I like metaphors, but similes are better. You and Jimmy are like a pair of rocks skipping."

She laughed. "Yes, Jimmy and I are like rocks skipping." This seemed to have broken her concentration.

"Jimmy's an artist with iron pans," he said.

She nodded, then looked him in the eyes. "You know how Kathleen likes to swim?"

"Kathleen? What about her?" He fiddled with his hearing-aid.

"Swimming... Kathleen..." were the only words he got.

"Kathleen likes to swim," said Ray.

Suzanne leaned closer to his ear with the hearing aid. "Yes, she did. Two days ago at her athletic club, Kathleen... drowned." Suzanne took a big breath. "Apparently she had an aneurysm that burst in her brain."

Ray felt he was falling, and he cupped his head. He realized he was safe in his chair. Would he black out? Suzanne's voice cracked, and she shook her head, saying, "I guess it was fast. A lifeguard got her out in seconds, but she was gone."

Suzanne now clasped him, and the light there in the sunroom grew brighter, blinding. He and his first wife had named their first child Kathleen for its Gaelic meaning, "pure little one."

Pure. Purity. Pureness. He didn't know if he said what he thought, but he wanted to say, "One's children aren't supposed to die before you." Kathleen, little bundle of tiny blankets, her bassinet so white, his wife breast-feeding for the first time, my little joy – why, why, why?

He now floated in the Milky Way, not in a spacesuit as George Clooney was in *Gravity,* arms and legs scratching for a foothold. No, Ray felt himself hovering as in a hot tub, buoyant, somehow seeing and breathing. The only problem was, the bearded Viet vet he'd given five dollars to on a street corner now drifted next to him with a full body, laughing. "Thanks for the money, man," said the man, whiskers white and long.

"Why are you here?" asked Ray.

Gordon, his former client from Scotland, floated in with a golf club. "Hoot, Mon!" said Gordon.

"Now come on," said Ray. "You're not really saying such a cliché thing, are you?"

"You brought us here," said Gordon. "Where would you rather be?"

Just like that, Ray returned to his Sonoma home, younger as he saw in the sunporch's mirror. Maybe he was sixty-five, Kathleen's age. The sun poked its face over the nearby mountains, casting pink on the overhead clouds, creating a strawberry parfait with the bluing sky. Soon the full sun gave a glamour-girl look to his grape vines, each leaf's edge highlighted with a golden color. A full moon floated in the sky just over the hills, opposite the sun. The valley, abuzz with the sound of flies, looked greener than he'd ever seen.

Right next to the house, the lawn's sprinklers burst on, offering umbrellas of wetness, filling the air with the revitalized scent of a recently mowed lawn.

A squirrel jumped from an oak branch onto his ruby-red barn, the squirrel's feet scurrying with the sound of loose chicklets.

At the window, the Siamese cat played with a fly that did not buzz.

The creak of a chair behind him made him twist around, and there he was in a hospital bed, rails up on the sides. Julie pulled the chair closer to the bed and took his hand, and she rubbed it as if it were Aladdin's lamp.

"Julie?" he said.

She didn't seem to hear him. She spoke to Suzanne, saying, "He's breathing faster. Does that mean something?"

He felt his other hand rubbed, and he turned. Suzanne struggled with a smile, gazing at him, her eyes glistening with tears. *Don't be sad,* he wanted to say as he felt strangely bright—and she nodded in release. Then he noticed: at the foot of the bed stood Suzanne's older half-sister, the departed Kathleen. She was as real as he remembered, wearing slinky dancing clothes as when she taught him the Cuban dance.

"Kathleen?" he said, and she padded over, offering her hand. Feeling limber, he pushed himself over a rail, stood up from the bed in his red pajamas, and took her hand. While there was no music, he and Kathleen grinned and, with a little Cuban action, stepped forward-forward-forward.

Incident on South Cecilia

"Solo Mayoreo," said the sign. Perhaps Carrie had wandered in here, even though Trevor knew the fabric store sold wholesale only, not open to the public. It looked dark in there, and a man at the door said in accented English, "This is for vendors only."

"My wife's a vendor," he said untruthfully. "I'm just looking for her."

The man directed him into the warehouse, and Trev's eyes adjusted from the intense sunlight on the street. From floor to nearly ceiling stood massive shelves filled with bolts of cloth from across the color spectrum, arranged by signs such as "cotton/algodón," "rayon/rayón," and "silk/seda." He couldn't help but think of how this might make a perfect episode for *Law and Order,* with the opening scene of a man's leg protruding from under a black bolt of seda.

Trev passed the head of each aisle, looking for Carrie in her stunning patterned black-and-white print dress. She'd designed and sewed it herself. She looked fantastic at thirty-five—ten years younger than he. So why did she disappear? She had to know he had nothing to do while waiting for her. Didn't she realize he had scripts to read, big decisions to make, as he did every weekend?

Earlier, Trev had sweated in the hot sun, watching his wife move from small store to small store in downtown Los Angeles, muttering that the cloth looked too florid and cheap. "Where's the stuff that Mood carries in West L.A. but less expensive?" she asked.

"Mood doesn't come down here. These are the cheap seats."

"You're being racist."

"How can I? I love Tijuana. Great place to drink."

"Right. As if you've been there."

"I have. I've seen the donkey show."

"Don't be gross," she said.

"Everything's cheap in downtown L.A.," he said. "Wholesale sunglasses are a few streets down."

"I just want to find the right black material."

Sewing was her new Buddha. She'd use such terms as "French seam" or "bias cut," and he'd come back at her with "Maguffin" or "magic hour," vocabulary used at the studio. He'd told her, however, he believed in her, which is why they had to go to the fashion district. He wanted this marriage to work. They'd hit the five-year mark.

"Why don't we walk on the other side of the street," he'd suggested. "That side has shade."

"You can," she said. "I'm doing this side first."

He hated her subtle power plays. To prove he wouldn't fall into that trap, he walked across the street to the shade. He paralleled her movements eastward on his side of the street. Once she entered a store, he became impatient and glanced into the window of a bargain-looking electronics store next to him. What were electronics doing in the fashion district? Mexican music blared from the open door. The digital cameras, MP3 players, and more had tiny signs next to them proclaiming *Venta!* Everyone loved a sale.

Trev knew Carrie wanted their next vacation to be to South America. Maybe after today, she'd rethink that. After all, she loved to travel in style. He'd been pushing for Denmark. He'd read a lot of great things about Copenhagen from a screenplay he once considered for production. It took place near Copenhagen's Tivoli Gardens.

He turned from the store, looked around at the throng of people on the sidewalks, then thought Carrie must still be in the store. He returned to the hot-sun side, hurried into the tiny store where he last saw her, but she'd evaporated.

Now in this warehouse, he thought it would be like her to go into this giant place closed to the public. She always carried herself as if she belonged wherever she was. She had never been to Los Angeles' fashion district, but in his attempt to have more "Carrie and Trev time," as their marriage counselor had called it, Trev had suggested they go to the fashion district. It would be their adventure, much as his own had been when he'd prepared his proposal to her by buying in downtown's jewelry district. A previous wife and a long-term girlfriend had taught him one thing: don't scrimp on the jewelry. He still loved bargains.

When he couldn't find her in the warehouse, sweat rolled from his forehead. He'd just call her cell and find out where she was, but he remembered she'd forgotten to charge her phone. His stomach knotted. Hell, she knew where the car was. She could meet him there. If nothing else, she could borrow someone's phone and call him, damn it. He'd go to the car now and run it with the air conditioner on. One car fucking idling wouldn't melt the polar ice cap.

He turned onto Cecilia Street, a long single alley-like block with stores on one side, and mostly wall on the other. A discarded Corona beer can lay on the sidewalk, and he kicked the goddamned trash into the street, thinking *venta!* The kickboxing that he learned for exercise at his club was good for something. He knew he had to deal with his anger better—don't take it out on Carrie, he told himself.

He spotted his green car halfway down at a meter on the wall side. Near a dumpster not far from his car, a young woman in a red tube top spoke angrily in Spanish to a tall thin man with a narrow beard, and the young man appeared to be taking every one of her words like a punch. Trev didn't understand a word, but he understood the subtext. She hadn't liked something he'd done. As she leaned in to punctuate some point, he slapped her face and yelled "Pucha!" She held her face and started crying. He was going to hit her again, when Trev shouted "Hey! No hitting women!" It was just like at the studio when he stopped two agents arguing. Trev ran closer, feeling the same surge he'd had with the can.

"Fuck off," said the young man in perfect English.

Trevor paused, his heart beating fast. "I don't like seeing what you did," he said.

"Then I should hit you," said the young man and took a swing.

Trev instinctively swiveled, surprised at the aggression. *Who's this fucking moron?* And without thinking, Trev let out a tremendous front kick, leaning into the kick as if the man were one of the seventy-pound punching bags at his club, directing the ball of his foot at the target. The flat of Trev's Danish boot smashed the young man in the chest, knocking him down.

On the ground, gasping for air, certainly surprised, the young man glared at Trev and again shouted "Pucha!"

Trev took that to mean an expletive, and he began kicking the young man harder and harder in the side, with the man saying, "No, stop!" and the young woman shouted, "Stop! Help!"

Yet his anger was such, Trev would show this young man not to hurt a woman again. He kicked harder.

"Stop!" yelled the woman.

"Trev?" he heard his wife shout, and as Trev turned, he saw Carrie, shocked and running toward him. At the same time, the woman he'd been protecting shouted something, and when he turned toward her, she was lunging at him. He felt a stab right into his chest. The young woman's frightened face was right near his. He looked down. Her hand left a pair of small orange-handled scissors sticking out of his chest. He was feeling faint.

The young man scrambled up and grabbed his girl-friend's hand. As Trev sank to the sidewalk, people gathered around. The couple ran off.

"You all right, señor?" said an old man. Then Carrie was at his side.

"Trev, what happened?" she said.

"I was protecting her."

"Who?"

He tried to point at the departing couple, but the pain was incredible in his chest, and he clenched his teeth so hard, he couldn't talk.

"Someone call an ambulance!" shouted Carrie.

He could feel himself blacking out. Why did relationships became harder after five years, he remembered thinking. Why couldn't people just have fun with each other? He and Carrie needed to have fun again.

Then he seemed to be dreaming about an ambulance, the driver saying something about "these fucking one-way streets in L.A." He opened his eyes to see a clear bag of some sort swinging on a pole above him. The bag had a clear thin tube leading to his arm, strapped near his side.

The sound of a siren was steady. And Carrie peered down at him.

"He's back!" she shouted to her right, and a blue-uniformed young man—a nurse? No, a paramedic—leaned over him and said, "How're you feeling, guy?"

"I'm a good husband," Trev said.

"Your blood pressure is back," he said, looking off to a monitor.

"Carrie," said Trev. "We should just have fun again, don't you think?"

"Yes, yes. How about once the doctors fix you up, we go to Copenhagen. Isn't that where you wanted to go?"

"It is. Tivoli."

"You can eat all the Swedish meatballs you want!" she said, happily.

"Copenhagen is in Denmark. Sweden is across the big bridge."

"Well, then, we'll cross that bridge."

He spent two days at Cedars Sinai hospital, where he'd been transferred at Carrie's insistence—they had the best Jewish doctors, she said. Carrie even slept in the same room with him on an armchair that turned into a futon. He'd never seen such devotion in her before.

"I can't be at home," she said. "What's Malibu without you?"

He spoke to his office, and he learned the film that he'd green-lighted, *Bring 'Em Back,* had to be delayed two weeks. It was a buddy picture about two Navy Seal single dads teaming up to parachute into Afghanistan. They needed to overthrow a tribal leader that had kidnapped one of their sons. The film's director was running over on another film. Trev's partner suggested to take a couple weeks off. "You wanted to go to Denmark, and your wife said she wanted to take you. Do it," he said. Carrie then arranged it.

On the plane across the aisle in the first-class section, Trev overhead an old couple chatting in what he knew to be Danish. The gentleman in an all-white suit looked much like Max von Sydow, the guy from Ingmar Bergman films but older as he was opposite Tom Cruise in *The Minority Report*. The man's wife looked a like another Bergman actress, Liv Ulman. The odd thing—maybe it was the mannerisms—but Trev could understand what they were saying. She was worried that his cancer wouldn't stay in remission, and he told her of all the things he had loved about her over the years, including her meatball recipe.

"Did you hear that?" Trev said to Carrie, dressed in an asymmetrical dress of her own design. He indicated the couple.

"They're talking in a foreign language," said Carrie. "What am I supposed to understand?"

"That we're on a journey where there are surprises."

"In Denmark?" she said.

He smiled and left it at that. She didn't get it.

They stayed at the Hotel D'Angleterre, where Hitchcock had filmed some of *Torn Curtain* with Julie Andrews and Paul Newman. The giant five-star white hotel, over 300 years old and sitting on Kongens Nytorv, the King's New Square, must have cost a lot, but it was a gift from Trev's partner. They stayed in the Karen Blixen suite, incredibly romantic with its African motif. Blixen had written *Out of Africa,* and who could forget Meryl Streep as Blixen in the film?

Trev found he made love as he had never before—never losing his hardness, and Carrie was happily experimental as she'd never been. She wanted to try as many positions as they could come up with.

That evening he wanted to eat a dinner based on the Oscar-winning foreign film *Babette's Feast,* which came from a story by Karen Blixen about a woman named

Babette who makes an incredible meal for remote villag-ers in Denmark in the 19ᵗʰ century. The food changes their lives. Trev had read that a Copenhagen restaurant had served the feast, but the hotel's concierge said the restaurant changed it to a meal inspired by the crime novel and movie *The Girl with the Dragon Tattoo*—small versions of all the eighteen sandwiches mentioned in the novel, with wine. They went for that.

The next day, Carrie was getting her hair done nearby and said she'd meet him in at a particular café in nearby Nyhavn, the New Harbor, not far from the hotel. He picked a table in the sun—it was cool, after all—and after he drank a few gulps of his Tuborg beer, he felt incredibly tired. He thought he'd lay his head on the table to sleep.

He was out when he felt Carrie tug him awake, and she yelled "Come on! We're late!" He wasn't sure what they were late for, but he ran after her, her beautiful black-and-white print dress from that day in Los Angeles rustling as they ran into the wind and onto a boat.

It was a large speedboat that might hold fifteen peo-ple, and when they got on, the boat took off down a canal very fast. It made him dizzy. Pastel-colored buildings whisked by. He didn't think Copenhagen had so many canals. It seemed more like Amsterdam, which he'd been to, and this all seemed strange. Now that he looked closer at Carrie, she didn't look like Carrie.

"Carrie? What happened to your face?"

"What do you mean?"

"It doesn't look like you. You look more like J.K. Rowling."

"Who's she?"

"The Harry Potter writer."

Carrie took her compact out of her purse to look at her face, but the mirror was missing. "I'm going to the bathroom," she said.

While she was gone, the boat pulled up alongside Tivoli Gardens, the famous amusement park, whose walls they'd seen when they came into the city from the airport by train. There were no canals next to Tivoli. How was this possible? And where was Carrie? Was she abandoning him again?

He wouldn't get off the boat until Carrie was back, but then the captain, who looked a lot like the captain from *Gilligan's Island,* was telling him that he must leave.

"I'm waiting for my wife. She's in the—what do you call it?—the water closet."

"No she's not," said the captain. He pointed down to the alley-like street with stores on one side and a wall on the other. There was Carrie in her black-and-white dress. She was hovering over someone who, as Trev ran closer, was a man completely horizontal and partly under a shroud of black silk with one leg jutting out. There in the center of his chest stood what looked to be orange-handled scissors.

Nestor by the Numbers

N estor walked with a bounce in his step past a hedge of bougainvillea bursting with red flowers. He stepped into the park, onto a flat grassy field, moving toward a circle of tall trees. His goal: the majestic oak at the front. It was here, more than twenty years earlier, where Nestor had proposed to Arabella using a hired Bozo—literally a clown in whiteface and red-ball nose. The clown had entertained her with a series of kazoos, slippery handshakes, and juggling balls, finally producing a ring on Nestor's behalf. She cried and said yes.

She was thirty-six then, and he, ten years older. Previously they had been married to others. Now today, on their anniversary, with their son at USC film school, she'd asked him to meet her here after work, there between Lake Hollywood and the Hollywood sign. Could she do something more surprising than a clown?

She emerged from an unfamiliar black Mercedes parked on the hill. Her dark shoulder-length hair fluttered in the breeze as she strode. Her tall and slender frame, still great looking after all these years, approached. He smiled at the sight of her. A man, the driver, stepped out, wearing a black turtleneck, a sports jack-

164 • The Benefits of Breathing

et, and silver hair. *Who is that guy?* he thought. *Like an ad for a sailing magazine.*

Arabella waved to Nestor, more like heiling Hitler than a happy hello, but perhaps it was the distance. The man trailed her. *Why is he coming?*

As she neared, Nestor stood and said "Hey," feeling ready for whatever surprise she had, something funny he hoped.

"Hi," said Arabella, feet away from him. He held out his arms. She did not move into them but said, "Sit, sit. I'll sit with you. This is Wolfgang." She pointed to the man, who had a close-cropped gray beard like an aged detective from *Miami Vice*. He held a thin briefcase, which he now snapped open. He produced a manila envelope and handed it to Nestor as Arabella sat.

"What's this?" Nestor said. Wolfgang had moved and appeared mostly as a silhouette, his silver hair a flag in the sun.

"As you know, anniversaries have not always been easy for me," said Arabella.

"Now, now," Nestor said to undercut any negativity. "This is a happy day and—"

"How about our seventh?" she said. "I'd told you then I'd never been with someone for over seven years. I didn't think I could do any more than that."

He'd remembered and recalled his laugh. "And I said we'd make it to twenty. Look. We did it." His truth was straight and true as the hummingbird that just buzzed by.

"We did it," she echoed, looking away.

"We made it. Next year will be our twenty-first. Three times seven is twenty-one, a lucky number. It's math." He followed her gaze. Was that a coyote in the hills? He said, "I have a reservation for us at the Smoke House, but I only made it for two." He again looked into the sun toward Wolfgang. "Should I make it for three?"

"Open the envelope," she said. "I know how much you like bookends, so this is a bookend."

He did. He caught on the first page the words "Petitioner: Arabella Fleetwood" and "Respondent: Nestor J. Aramakis"

"What is this?" he said, reading further. "A joke? It's not very funny."

"You're a really nice guy—"

"Now come on now!"

"And we have a beautiful son together. Yet Wolfgang is my lover. He is also my divorce attorney, and he's serving you papers."

Lover? She has a lover? He couldn't speak.

"I know this is a rather formal way of doing things, but—"

"What's happening?" Nestor said, frowning, trying to understand.

"I can't suffer anymore," she said. "I'm getting out of this trap. You just seem to be on autopilot."

"We're happy. What're you talking about? We don't have big fights."

"This isn't a big fight, either," she said.

And that was that. She moved out two days later.

Slowly, over months, seeing a therapist twice weekly, occasionally visiting with Arabella, their attorneys, and a divorce mediator, he came to accept this dissolution. He accepted he was alone and lost the love of his life. She was his love, right? He would ask himself wouldn't his true love be there for him? She wasn't there.

There's a blackness to a lost love that years/songs/movies/teardrops have tried to capture, but when you're in a loss, breathing is hard, and crying does nothing but squeeze every water molecule out of you—and you're still alive. He endured. Waking up, he'd feel spacey for a few moments, okay even, then he'd realize he had the whole day ahead of him.

If only he could torch the sky.

He told himself he wouldn't use the box of Kleenex that his therapist, Rosemary, placed on the couch, but he grabbed sheets by the boxcar load and stained them, poor pathetic man that he was.

Rosemary, patient, empathetic, good-natured, had come highly recommended from another VP at Warner Bros. Rosemary started slowly, just trying to get him to talk. A stout woman with the optimism of a newlywed, she was a good listener. One of her questions on their third meeting was "Do you ever read poetry?"

He said, "Arabella once gave me a book of poems by Billy Collins. Pretty good stuff for poetry. Arabella used to write poems. I never knew what to say other than 'That's really good, honey.' I think she wanted me to be more critical."

"I only ask," said Rosemary, "because you should try writing poetry. Because it's so condensed, it makes you think and feel. I want you to feel. Be honest. Be true. Sometimes you'll find surprises."

The next day, pen in hand, he sat before a blank page of paper. The paper was so white. What if he cut open a vein and bled all over it? That's what he really wanted to say. What would that be in words? How was he supposed to do this? All he knew was the truth. He wrote one thing:

MORNINGS IN A QUIET HOUSE

In the morning,
I clean the cat box,
I 409 the kitchen,
I pour kibble into a cat bowl,
I sweep the stairs.
I do all the things you once did,
And I wonder what you miss about me.

"Nothing" spills from my lips.
Maybe there's something,
But I won't know.
The fact I kissed you
every night
before sleep,
or brought you San Francisco Fog coffee
in the morning, or once carried
our son on my shoulders,
or watched scary movies with you
even though you know I hate scary movies
and snakes on a plane
and sharknadoes –
maybe that made you smile?

Now I live in a scary movie.

I realize how you prepared me.

At the next session, after he'd read it to Rosemary, she clapped her hands and said, "You're a writer. Wow! Now I'm hearing how you feel. It's okay to feel sad. To be human is, at times, to be sad. It's all right. Accept it. You're opening up, and that's good."

Later, he realized the poem was laughable and useless. Pitiable. He didn't grow up to be pitiable. Get it together, man. Stop being weak and absurd. How could he stop his brain? Well, there was one way. No. He wouldn't go there.

As if the weather matched him, December became gray. It rained. Often. Long and hard.

He 409'd the whole house.

Arabella was generous, letting him have the house. Was that generous? Wouldn't have staying together been more generous?

"What's the connection between people, exactly?" he asked Rosemary at the next session. "Can love be measured in volts? In revolutions per minute?"

"The intangible can't be measured," she said. She looked reassuringly at him from her easy chair. She seemed ageless. He tried to guess her age. Mid-forties? Certainly younger than he. Wise people seemed ageless. He sat on the wide, cloth-covered couch.

"And trust is what? A shoelace that can snap in two?" Nestor said. "A bird's nest built in a chimney? A set of monkey bars that electrocutes you when a lightning bolt comes by?"

She laughed. She had such energy in it. He loved making her laugh. "Yes, you were broadsided," she said. "But you need better thinking."

"That's why I'm here."

"Good," she said. "Some relationships have expiration dates. You're trying to find the exact cause and how to blame her. It's wasted energy. Move on."

"To a life of loneliness?" he asked.

"Why do you say that with such a smile on your face?"

"Sometimes I wonder if I'm mature. Sixty-six, and I haven't grown up?" He took in the smell of incense, sandalwood.

"Do you want to be alone?" she asked.

"No."

"What's wrong with being alone? Why do you want to be with someone?"

He felt vulnerable and exposed with such a question, and he pondered. He finally said, "I read about a young woman, twenty-three, an Olympic athlete in cycling. She won an Olympic silver medal, and she was going to be in the next Olympics. She killed herself by breathing an inert gas. In the note she left behind, she said all she wanted was to feel loved and connected. Isn't that what we all want?"

"Yes, loved and connected. But kill yourself if you're alone and can't get it?"

"I've been alone plenty of times in my life. Having a partner is better. Except now that I have two ex-wives, I feel pathetic."

"Let's remain positive. What's a good marriage, a good relationship, to you?"

"It's like being Butch and Sundance—or Butch and Emma. You're just good together. You experience things together that no one else does, like jumping off a cliff into a river and surviving. You're a single unit with two brains. You create memories that only you two get."

"Beautiful."

"It's two people helping each other through life. Life can be otherwise brutal."

She smiled and nodded, then looked at him earnestly. "It's time for you to start dating. You need to put yourself out there. Talk with women."

"Men my age don't date," he'd said emphatically.

"Yes, they do. They use online services the most. Men in their sixties, women in their fifties. There's a sea of single people."

"Using Match dot com?"

"A few other services I recommend, too."

She would later email him a short list. Rosemary then urged him to date at least two women at once "because from your history, you bond easily. I need you to stay objective. Dating more than one woman at a time will keep you objective."

"I've never done that; I can't," he said. "It's just not moral. I've never even cheated on anyone."

"You're not pledging exclusivity at the start. No one does. See if you can have fun."

"Is that why we're here—to have fun and then die?"

"Geez, Nestor. Relax a little. It's not about sealing a deal. It's just having a coffee or a dinner."

"Yeah?"

"You need to meet a variety of women, get a bigger overview than you ever have. Stay in the present. Don't dwell on the past or anticipate the future. Live in the now."

"Sounds like a fortune cookie."

She laughed. "You're not buying a new car. This is about connection. Can you simply talk with your date, enjoy each other? See two people a week if you can. Have no goal other than some pleasant talk. Learn about others."

"Okay, I'll think about dating," he said.

He continued to work on his animated Warner show, *Green Lantern Finds the Light,* now streaming. He ate dinner with his son, Josh, at least once every two weeks – downtown as there just wasn't a great place to eat near USC.

On the next Saturday, Josh told him that his mother had recently moved from her apartment into Wolfgang's wooded view house on Mulholland Drive. "It's a really great place," Josh said with enthusiasm. "Like some of the shots in the David Lynch film, *Mulholland Drive.* You see the dots of light in a grid pattern in the Valley. Gorgeous."

"I never understood that film," said Nestor.

"It's about dreams. In the film, the protagonist Diane lives in a drug-induced stupor where she imagines she gets her career and the girl she loves. She kills herself, though. Did you get that?"

"I like straight narratives. The guy gets the girl. They're happy. No suicides." Nestor picked at his chicken enchilada and said, "My therapist said I should start dating."

"That's a good idea, Dad. I recommend using Tinder."

"I know about Tinder," said Nestor. Josh's USC roommate, Georgi from Bulgaria, had told Nestor about Tinder, which a lot of young people used. You choose your basic parameters—such as age range of your date and miles you're willing to drive—and you are given photos of potential dates, one at a time. You swipe right if you found them attractive and swipe left if you didn't. After that, you go through the good choices, find out more about them, and send them messages. Your choices then receive your message with your picture and basic profile, too. Supposedly, Josh was a Tinder master, meeting women often, mostly for sex for a date or two before moving on.

"Tinder is not for me," said Nestor. "It's for people who aren't serious and don't want a connection. What films are you going to make if there's no connection?"

"School is like fifteen hours a day, Dad. I don't have time for something serious. Did you really connect with Mom? You always seemed busy."

"Maybe I made mistakes," Nestor said.

Nestor's house—now that he'd signed the papers, it was all his—stood in the Atwater Village section of L.A., not far from the house in *Pulp Fiction* where drug dealer Lance lived, the guy who supplied the adrenaline injected into Mia Wallace's heart to save her. The neighborhood was a little more upscale now. It wasn't far from Griffith Park, where the observatory looked into the universe to find its secrets.

Nestor went to Match.com just to look. The first time, he spent less than fifteen seconds on it. He just wasn't ready. The second time, the next day, he clicked on "View Singles" after giving his birthdate. He saw some possibilities. The third time, he saw more women and a discount offer to try the site for three months. It wasn't free, but it was reasonable.

He had to enter a lot of his information. He worked hard and long on a profile, going to Google to search for "How to write a good profile for Match.com." He learned to be honest and specific. A few sample profiles gave him a clear understanding: don't try to be someone false because women read subtext better than men.

It was like writing an essay for college—his hopes and dreams filtered in there as well as his passions. He loved specific restaurants and foods, such as the Cuban garlic chicken at Versailles and the chicken enchiladas and strawberry margaritas at El Coyote. Music remained important to him, such as albums by Joni Mitchell and Pink Floyd, and he loved skiing and swimming but was open to trying new things. When he was done with that, he put in as his search criteria: women in their fifties and living within five miles of him.

The site gave him twelve women's pictures and profiles as possible matches. He studied each one, and each time, he tried to imagine spending the rest of his life with this person. He couldn't picture that with any of the dozen. Some profiles seemed simply surface with sentences like, "I love dancing and trying new foods and walking on the beach hand-in-hand with my soulmate, who is not afraid of anything."

It sounded too much like a *Playboy* playmate profile – but then again, maybe that appealed to men's fantasies. Would those men be looking at women in their fifties? They'd want women in their twenties, but young women would still be choosing majors. He wanted someone who'd experienced the same culture as he had.

A couple of the women's profiles seemed more like rants. "I want someone faithful. I'm not looking for a man with a wandering eye or someone who cannot commit. I'm not looking for a guy who's quick to criticize others, such as friends, a waitress, or me. If you're on Match for a one-night stand, please pass me by. I also want someone with good hygiene who knows how to use a toothbrush, takes showers, and washes his hands after using the bathroom."

Yikes. Men could be beasts, he supposed, but all these negatives were a turnoff. Where was the person open to meeting new people and simply enjoying that?

He did like one woman's pictures and profile. She was with her adult son in one photo and on horseback in another. He loved horseback riding—he'd forgotten that. He hadn't done it in years. Maybe he'd contact her.

Now he was stumped. How was he to contact her? There was a button for "like," another for a wink, and a third for "favorite." Was a wink better than a like? How could someone be a favorite if you haven't even talked with her? Would she then write him?

When he clicked on "like," a window popped up, suggesting he write a short note, too, and the window offered a space to write. One was likely to get a response when writing a good note.

The woman didn't have a real name, though. She was listed as "LovelyInLA." All the women had similar handles, such as DustyFun and BridleBeach. He was listed just as "Nestor."

He wrote, "Dear LovelyinLA: I'm new to this, and I don't understand really what I'm supposed to do—wink, "like," or both? Anyway, what you write about is interesting. I loved summer camp, too, lo, many years ago. I still feel like a kid. –Nestor." That seemed a good first attempt. He clicked on Send.

He heard back from her later that day: "Dear Nestor. I've been on Match for a couple of years, and I can say women tend to use "like" or a wink, while guys write a note as you did. I looked at your profile. My ex-husband was in the film industry as you are, and I don't want to see anyone from the film industry ever again – too obsessive. Good luck."

So much for #1.

Late that day, two women who looked like models in their twenties each selected him as a "favorite" but had no notes. Each looked as if they'd hired professional photographers, offering photos revealing their cleavage and tight bodies. They were also from other states. One was from Seattle, and the other was from Oklahoma. He guessed they were either a scam or women looking for a rich sugar daddy. He was annoyed at this.

The next morning when he had another gorgeous woman in Florida wink at him, he wondered if he just wasted his money by using Match.com. Then a woman from Texas who was thirty-seven with a couple of amateurish pictures—good looking but not stunning—sent a short note: "I like Cuban food, too. Particularly black beans." While her handle was "PatrioticGal," she signed her note as Gretchen.

Now this really irritated him. He wrote back immediately.

"Dear Gretchen, I'm new to online dating, but what I don't get is I said I'm looking for someone in her fifties and within five miles of Hollywood. You are neither. And how could I have coffee with you if you're in Texas?"

He received a reply within minutes. "Nestor, I hope I didn't upset you. I'm not in Texas but in Afghanistan where I'm serving in the Army as a medical assistant. My tour of duty ends next month as does my career in the Army. I've hit twenty years, so I can get a pension, and I want to retire to Los Angeles."

She can retire at thirty-seven? He read on:

"Because I'm retiring, I'm looking for someone older, near retirement, so we can have fun together and travel. That's why I wrote you. Attached are three more photos. I hope you write me back. Let's use our own email instead of Match's as I lost a whole note to you when I went to another screen.

"Mine is: Gretchen.Blackwell0923@gmail.com. Gretchen."

All three photos showed her in an Army uniform. These were not glamour shots, and they showed her as thin and dark-haired, but not unattractive. The uniform certainly wasn't sexy.

He wrote her back using his email to her address. "Gretchen, I'm just too new at this. I can't write after this as you're too far away, and I'm too newly separated. Maybe I shouldn't be on Match, truthfully. Good luck to you! Nestor."

That evening, he received another note from her. "Nestor, no rush! I'm just trying to get to know you. I know your *favrit* food, but what else do you like to do for fun? The food in the chow hall here is better than you might *aspect*. We even have Papa John Pizza. I feel I've served my country well. Now I just want to settle down with the *rite* guy. Your profile seems very *interasting* to me."

Yikes. She misspelled four words—too much in a hurry or not a good education? He shouldn't have written her. He'd make it clear now: "Dear Gretchen. Thank you for helping our country. You probably should look for another Army person who could understand you. We are not a match. Good luck!" He didn't sign his name this time.

It was another day before he heard from her again. "Dear Nestor. I feel I should tell you more about myself so you can see me more clearly. I would love to learn more about you, too, such as your *favrit* song and color.

"I have spent a lot of time on this note because it's important. I'm not looking for an Army guy because at one point, I ended up sleeping with my former captain and got pregnant by him. I had the baby, Priscilla, and she's in a foster home in New York.

"When I retire next month, I'm going to pick her up and move to Los Angeles, where I had grown up in foster care. My parents had been killed in a car crash when I was eight. If you give me your address, I'll give that to my commanding officer for my discharge papers, and Priscilla and I can come to your home. In the meantime, we'll get to know each other by email, and then we'll be like best friends when I arrive. How's that? Please tell me more about *yerself*."

Now his heart pounded, and he quickly reread his other notes to her to see if he'd given any personal information where she could find him. He'd given his email address, nothing else. He went to Google and searched for "Match.com scams and safety."

Match.com itself had safety tips. Do not ever ever ever send anyone money, no matter how flattering he or she is to you and no matter how "real" the need seems. There are many scammers out there.

On another link, he read of six red flags to look for in online dating, and the first was moving off site to personal email. Nestor had fallen for that.

On another link, he read about a high-powered thirty-six-year-old female attorney, Irene, who had fallen quickly for a guy named Sean Ellis Bradford. He was honest, loving, and very rich. He drove a Jaguar and wore tailored suits much like Sean Combs. He worked for the CIA, he said, so he could not disclose a lot about his work, but it had to do with tracking wealth outside of the country. She had introduced Bradford to her friends and family right away. They all loved him.

About to build a $25-million home in Beverly Hills, Bradford had not yet broken ground, but Irene saw the wooded site, saw his plans, and he wanted her to live there with him. She met with his architect, who said they were nailing down a contractor to start the work. Bradford said it wasn't too late to change the plans if she saw something missing or wrong. She felt the pool should include a hot tub, and he completely agreed. After that, he whisked her off for four amazing days to New York City where they saw two plays and made love for hours.

In short, she'd been through a bitter divorce two years earlier, and this guy was everything her husband had not been: attentive, suave, stylish, and loving. After two more weeks, Bradford proposed to her with an impressive diamond ring, and she said "Yes!"

In another two weeks, she was pregnant with his baby. It was only after she drained her savings for him— $250,000 to help pay his lawyers involved with unlocking his frozen funds and to get the house started on time—that she miscarried. She then found in the trunk of his Jaguar his car's registration wedged underneath the spare tire. The car was registered to another name.

While she had earlier used Google to search for people named Sean Ellis Bradford, none of the pictures matched her guy. Of course, he said. For his job, he couldn't use social media. When she later typed in the name she found on his car's registration, there was a lot on this guy, dubbed the Casanova Con, with a jailhouse photo of her lover. He must have picked up on her discovery as his car disappeared, and he never showed up again. He sent one email saying he loved her and was in

Switzerland for work. Her diamond ring turned out to be fake. She had a complete breakdown that sent her to the hospital. She said that she had felt raped—emotionally, financially, and physically.

This story made Nestor instantly sick to his stomach. Had his identity been stolen or had Gretchen somehow gotten more information that would lead to his bank accounts being drained? His Gretchen was probably some guy in a tiny office in the San Fernando Valley using images off the internet, trolling for desperate guys with money.

He wrote Gretchen back instantly. "Good news! My wife returned. We are not divorcing. Sorry, but you and Priscilla cannot stay with me. My wife and I are working hard to make this work this time. You seem like a good person. May you find the right guy."

Within an hour, she wrote, "I'm sad for me but happy for you. I wish you the best. You seem like a good guy."

Whew. He never wrote her again. He reported this scam to a link on Match.com, including her handle name and the emails she had sent him. The next day, he received a note back saying, "Match has investigated this person. She has violated our rules of conduct, so we have removed her. Thank you for calling this to our attention."

So much for #2. This online dating thing was terrible. He didn't like the fact that Match was a magnet for such people. Still, if he could avoid the scammers, it had to be better than meeting people in bars.

He unenrolled in Match. He investigated other sites that Rosemary had given him and joined a specialty dating site, Ellington International, which focused on professionals meeting professionals. The website said, "Take your happiness and love life as seriously as your career." It was much more expensive than Match, but he figured that would weed out scammers. He joined. He used his same profile, but looked at his verbs, avoiding "am" and "is" and using more active verbs such as "enjoy" and "cherish."

Ellington International had its parameters page. Like Match, there were all sorts of checkable boxes for what he wanted in an ideal date, including driving time. He wanted thirty minutes or less.

The boxes came with a warning – that the more you checked, the fewer your choices. He checked "skiing." Someone who skied would be great. Skiing was gliding through a landscape, which always felt like a dream. How fun would it be to dream again with someone?

Before he had a chance to try out a selection, however, a little "ding" went off on his laptop. He had an email from an Ellington member already, his third interaction overall, Woman #3, named Sharon. He clicked on photos and her biography. She had a smile as wide as the Mississippi, and gorgeous auburn hair.

The CEO of a small clothing company in the fashion district downtown, fifty-two years old with a teenage daughter, Sharon wrote that a girlfriend had prodded her to try out Ellington. She loved to see the stars at night, vacation in Greece, and enjoyed rock concerts, especially Coldplay. More photos showed her in low-cut blouses—clearly she had assets there—and yet she appeared elegant, a lot like the blonde in the executive chair on the homepage of Ellington.

He clicked on the email. It said, "Dear Nestor. I love your name. Is it Greek? I saw in your profile you loved to eat at La Pergoletta in Los Feliz. I love that place. I live nearby in Atwater. Love the affogato. Do you know it?" She signed "hugs, Sharon."

Hugs. How wonderful was that? Maybe she would be Lucky Number 3 for him. After all, she lived in Atwater. What if he could walk to her place?

Affogato! He loved affogato and wrote her back: "Sharon, affogato is vanilla ice cream in espresso coffee! We should all be in espresso coffee. Affogato rules!"

She suggested they meet at La Pergoletta.

It was as simple as that? He said he was free the day after tomorrow. She said, "Deal. How's 7 p.m.?"

As he drove there at the appointed time, he wondered if he'd been too quick. Shouldn't they have talked on the phone first, or written more emails? Does she have a sense of humor? And because she had a clothing company, what did he know about fashion? He'd mix stripes with plaids. His son told him once when he wore a brown belt with his black shoes that his belt needed to be black to match his shoes.

"What's wrong with brown?" he'd said. "Brown and black go together, no?"

"No," Josh said. "It's simple."

So Nestor had his black belt with his black shoes—and his black pants and black shirt. And he drove his white car. Was that a fashion faux pas?

He pulled up to the restaurant in a strip mall. One spot was left—a good sign? Would he recognize her? He turned off the car and thought, *This is a really bad idea.* It was as if he were cheating on Arabella. He wasn't ready. What would his therapist say if he didn't go in and just meet? Okay, he'd try it.

As soon as he stepped in, a woman by herself at a table by a window waved. She looked.... Great! That was her. Her wide smile was genuine. She looked down at her hands a moment as if having doubts. Did she have doubts? Her thick hair fell with a curl to her yellow jacket and flowery blouse. She looked back up with reassurance. He smiled.

"Nestor," she said as he stepped closer, and when he nodded, she stood, smiling more. They hugged. This was better.

As soon as he sat, he saw the menus were already there. "Am I late?" he asked.

She looked at her elegant gold watch and said, "You're a minute early. That's nice."

"Listen," he said, "I've never, you know... I mean, I've dated, but not for about twenty-some years."

"Twenty-four for me," she said, looking relieved. "If I'm a little bumbling, it's just I'm rusty."

"You haven't been going out with new guys every week?" he asked.

"I've never done this before."

He placed his hand on his heart. "I feel more comfortable already."

"Same here," she said with relief. They smiled at each other as if they were reunited friends—then both looked at their menus to fill the silence.

A waiter, a thin young woman with a black apron, came over, asking, "May I get anything for you to drink? Wine? Beer?"

"Chianti?" they both said at the same instant. Nestor glanced at Sharon in a new way, impressed.

"We're samers," she said.

"A bottle of chianti?" asked the waiter. "Or two glasses?"

"A bottle of your best," said Nestor. He turned to Sharon. "It's on me, by the way. I'm old-fashioned, and I just can't stand the thought of anything different."

"Thank you," she said.

They again looked at their menus. He thought the *filetto in padella,* steak with garlic and rosemary olive oil, looked good. "Are we supposed to talk about our pasts?" he asked. "I'm not sure how this works."

"I'm happy to talk about anything. I love my past. I was in love right until my husband, Frank, died."

"Died?" He didn't know Sharon was a widow. She'd said nothing about that in her profile.

"At Morton's Steak House." She looked right at him, not upset. "At first, I thought he was choking on steak. He just fell right onto his mashed potatoes."

"He choked on steak?"

"People screamed. A surgeon, having dinner next to us, tried to do the Heimlich... Poor Frank was already dead. It was a brain tumor that did it." She looked at the next table over, as if it had happened there. An older couple looked at her, then got back to eating.

"So you're not divorced?" Nestor asked.

"Didn't I tell you?" she said. "His doctors told us that with his brain tumor, he could go in a flash like that." She snapped her fingers, revealing her painted blue nails. "But we didn't believe it'd be that quick, for some reason. It's sort of like the end of *The Sopranos,* right? The screen that suddenly goes black?"

"Tony Soprano died? That's what the black screen meant?"

She nodded. "Our daughter still struggles a lot with her father's death. None of her friends have lost a parent."

"How old is she?"

"Fifteen. Her father adored her—a really perfect dad."

He thought, *I can't compete with a perfect, dead guy. And such a dramatic ending.*

The dinner went well, although he didn't get the steak. He tried pasta with garlic and olive oil instead. You can't choke on that. Soon, he didn't worry about Sharon's widowhood or her daughter. He and Sharon learned they each had dogs. She suggested they walk their dogs together sometime in Griffith Park. "I'd love to do that," he said.

Two days later, their dogs, both small, hers a corgi, his, a white bichon, liked each other and walked side-by-side. For a third date, he suggested a movie. They saw a weekend matinee of an old movie, *Lawrence of Arabia,* playing at the Egyptian Theater. They talked for two hours afterward, getting wine next door at the Pig and Whistle.

When he brought her home, he remembered from his younger years that if you didn't kiss by the third date, then it wouldn't work out. He felt the moment was right and kissed Sharon at her front door. As he leaned in, she seemed surprised, but then she responded well. He even felt her tongue. They stood there like teenagers for a moment, each looking from the ground to each other's eyes. "Well," he said. "That was nice."

"Yes. 'Nothing is written,'" she said, quoting Lawrence from the movie. "Thank you for the great evening." She turned and walked into her house without looking back. Her corgi stared at him from the front door until the door closed.

She called two days later. "Nestor, you're a really nice man."

Oh, oh, he thought. *This isn't a good start.*

"Yesterday was the second anniversary of my husband's death," she said, "and it brought up a lot of stuff for me and my daughter. I met with my therapist to talk it out. I thought I was ready to date, but once I started liking you, I started feeling guilty. It's not fair to you."

Number 3, Number 3, don't do this to me.

"I'm not ready for a relationship or a boyfriend," Sharon said.

"I was the opposite," he said immediately. "I thought I wasn't ready, but then I was. My instincts are good—that you're a great person—and I really hoped to know you more. If it was about that kiss—"

"No, not at all. It was a nice kiss. I'm sorry. That's all I can say. This is what my therapist told me. I'm not ready."

Who was he to argue with a therapist? "Okay. Thank you," he said.

Nestor met with Rosemary the next day and gave the details of the three dates with Sharon. "I really liked her. I thought this could be it. She listens, she's funny, she's vulnerable. I like her."

"And did you set up dates with anyone else?"

He looked at her, puzzled. "Why would I?"

"I told you that you needed more objectivity. Look at you, ready to have a relationship with the first woman you meet."

"Destiny may be at work."

"Destiny is just a porno name," she said. "There is no destiny."

"T.E. Lawrence might agree with you. He said, 'Nothing is written.'"

"Exactly," she said. "People will be a part of your history, but it's not destiny—just as it wasn't destiny that drove Arabella away. Psychological needs are different from destiny."

"To me," said Nestor defensively, "destiny is in people's personalities. Each person has a personality that doesn't really change. Who you see is who you get. Thus, they will do what they do—like Arabella was bound to leave me, but I didn't see the clues."

"I'll agree with you that people have personalities. But being a widow is not a personality."

"How you respond to trauma is."

"And you're responding well, by the way, because you seem willing to understand, to learn—to change."

"Maybe."

"Traumas can be overcome. What I'm trying to get you to do is be more objective and open-minded. Learn from the women you date. You're not in Human Resources looking to fill the position of wife. Be with each person. Learn from each one."

"Learn? What's to learn?"

She laughed heartily. "Stop looking for 'the one' or the idea someone is your destiny. This is about choice. I want you to simply be in the present moment and see what you learn." He nodded.

"And when online dating, set up at least two people in a week—more if you can handle it. Is that a deal?"

"Deal," he said, and he went back to Ellington International where he hadn't been for over a week. The website had created a list of ten possible women. Ten! As he watched a Netflix movie, Nestor looked at each woman's profile. The movie was about how a beautiful girl's rich Brazilian father abandoned her in America with no credit cards. She gets help from a cleaning woman, finds a rich guy, and marries him—a perfect film for reading dating profiles. Of the ten, he found five were possibilities as they lived fairly close. He sent them notes and within hours, heard back from two. After a few more exchanges, he had dates with each.

The first, whom he dubbed Number 4, owned four big apartment buildings in Westwood around UCLA— probably each a goldmine for the constant flow of students willing to pay top dollar. Her pictures online were cute—curly hair and a cheerleader smile. He suggested a steakhouse he knew, and when they met, she had him laughing in no time with how clueless students were these days. "I mentioned to one guy who wanted to rent from me that he looked like a young Mick Jagger," she said. "The guy never heard of Jagger or the Rolling Stones. What planet are we on?"

Still, Nestor instantly had wondered about her age, as she looked older than her pictures. When he learned both of her parents had been Nazi concentration camp survivors, and they had learned their parenting methods in the camp—using whips— he instantly thought she might have issues.

"What year were you born?" he asked.

"Ah. The age issue. I knew it would come up." She was seven years older than she'd put on the website—a dating specialist she'd hired had told her to do so as guys didn't want to date women in their sixties. He didn't call her again. A relationship couldn't start with a lie. Still, he realized humor was a key ingredient.

Number 5 was the CEO of a chain of children's afterschool care centers in Hancock Park and South Pasadena, two upscale communities. They met in Hollywood at Yamashiro, a great Japanese restaurant on a hill. After a couple of drinks, she ranted how her ex-husband used her for money, and she left him at considerable cost. With another two drinks, she revealed how she once got so drunk in Oklahoma that her boyfriend beat her up and put her in the hospital for three days. Nestor didn't call her back after that. He didn't like heavy drinkers.

His dating site gave him another ten possibilities, and he culled them down to three, and each responded positively to his emails. One was a psychologist who ran her own firm with four other family-and-marriage counselors. Another was a lawyer in a big law firm downtown, and the third was a doctor.

The psychologist, Number 6, pleasant on the phone, was humorless in person when they met at Langer's Deli downtown, near her office, across from MacArthur Park. She spoke about her ex-husband the whole time and said, "These days, we're supposed to have these equitable marriages, and women can be as successful as they want to be. But nobody told the men that we got permission for that!" Then she went into her ex's sexual needs. Nestor felt that if he had a cake, he would want to leave it out in the rain.

He met the lawyer, Number 7, at a fancy French restaurant called the Perch downtown, on the fifteenth-floor terrace, a place that she had suggested. At dinner, she bragged how she charged $600 an hour and that "law was all about billable minutes." After he'd told her a story about meeting Robin Williams for a possible role in his animated show, she glanced at her watch. He figured his story took up at least $100 of her time. She told him they didn't match but thanks for dinner. All right.

The next day, he considered what the hell he was doing. Was this really the way to find love and connection?

Maybe he should think of dating like going to a gift shop. Most such stores, like the ones on Hollywood Boulevard, overflowed with stupid things, such as curvy

Hollywood starlet candleholders, "I ♥ LA" T-shirts, or a California license plate with your first name on it. Then you might find in some forgotten corner something truly beautiful, such as stained glass made for a Frank Lloyd Wright house. Dating was finding the great glass.

He saw the doctor, Number 8, at a Thai restaurant on Sunset, near where she worked at Kaiser as a chief of cardiology. There, he learned she'd been married twenty years to another doctor who had become obsessive about many things, including taking out the garbage with a surgical mask and latex gloves on and avoiding sex for all the potential bacteria he might encounter. She'd waited eight years until her kids were in college before divorcing him.

He liked her, Dr. Bonnie, and while she took his offered hand at an art gallery on their third date, she didn't look the least interested in kissing. He mentioned this to his therapist Rosemary, who said, "Maybe your rule for kissing by the third date should be relaxed. She has potential."

By their sixth date, they still hadn't kissed, so he brought this up at dinner. She said, "I really like you, Nestor, but I'm not really looking for more than a friend." He didn't ask her why she was on a dating site. He just stopped seeing her. Still, he had learned patience with her and understood the pressures of her job. She typically lost at least one patient a day—and more if you included other lost patients in her department.

He dated two other women while seeing Bonnie. Number 9's pictures seemed down-to-earth, as if she wasn't trying to impress anyone. Her eyes seemed honest. She, Milena, owned her own insurance agency in Glendale, was divorced, Armenian, and a mother. She skied.

They met at the Beachwood Café, which was close to him and was quaint like a diner in a small town. In person, Milena was chunkier than her pictures online. She was twenty years younger than him, too, younger than he meant to date, but Rosemary had said to date as young as forty because "after forty, everyone's really the same age."

Milena showed him pictures of her two young sons, butterball boys about to enter their teens. "Nice," he said. Couldn't he be more descriptive than that? They looked broken, loss wrapping around them like bacon around a hot dog. He kept silent.

Milena said her husband had absolutely no drive, had lived off of her, and was a lazy dad. When she discovered he had a cocaine problem, she left him, but technically, they hadn't divorced, to keep him on her health plan.

There were too many problems there, Nestor saw. That was a one-date event. He said, "Sorry, Milena, but my wife came to the house this morning, said she wanted to come back. I haven't said yes, which is why I didn't cancel this, but now I'm thinking she and I will make it work." It wasn't true. She hadn't come back, but he thought it would soften the blow for Milena. "Good luck," he said. "You deserve someone good."

Number 10 was unplanned. He'd joined a ski club to get away once in a while. The club rented an elegant bus with TV screens every four rows to let them watch movies. The bus carted forty members on the five-hour drive to Mammoth. As it pulled out from the Van Nuys Flyaway bus station one Friday evening, coolers with beer, wine, and sandwiches swung open, and it became a party bus.

Many of the members had been in the club for years, and many were in their seventies, spry, fun, and funny. By now, Nestor was used to meeting new people, so he soon felt a part of those standing at the back of the bus as they regaled him with stories of previous ski trips, particularly of members who had now passed away.

On the slopes the next morning, he began by following the oldest ones in the club up a long chairlift to what he thought would be an easy slope. With two black double diamonds, the sign at the top said, "Warning! Experts Only!" Another sign said, "Beware. Fast snow."

The oldsters zipped over the edge as if it were nothing. As he peered down the slope, it seemed more like a cliff. Without another mountain across the way, he also felt as if he were high in an airplane. He hated heights. It's what he'd always battled in skiing.

He heard a groan behind him, and a woman in a stylish orange ski suit stood, looking petrified. "Do you think we can take the chair back down?" she asked him in a Russian accent.

"No. No one can put us on the lift down. We have to ski."

"Damn it," she said, pulled out a silver flask, and drank from it. She held it out to him, saying, "Liquid courage. It's not a good day to die."

"No thanks. The trick, I think, is making the first turn. Once you see you can do it, the rest should be easy."

She shuddered. "Death is a giant against whom even the Tsars must draw weapons."

He laughed and remembered her from the bus, Tatiana, sexy, brash, confident, funny. She'd come from Moscow over twenty years ago and married a Brazilian soccer player who now had a big job at Neutrogena, a company specializing in skin care products.

"Follow me," Nestor said, not believing he just said it.

"Okay," she said.

Shit. He moved to the edge and, without pausing, pushed himself over. Everything became as terrifying as he expected, and he plunged faster than he wanted, his ski jacket flapping. His feet knew what to do, though, and he turned first right, then left. By the sixth turn, he actually liked the hill. It felt as if he were the star of his own ski movie. He could hear the swish of Tatiana behind him. They passed four club members getting up from the snow, laughing. They'd fallen but were okay.

When he reached the bottom of the steepest section, he stopped, and Tatiana's sharp edges bit to a stop just behind him. When he looked, she held her poles straight up and shouted. "We survived! Thank you!"

She invited him to lunch at McCoy Lodge, halfway up the mountain, and she paid. He learned she was ten years younger than he was, had two adult children, and was separated from her husband, who had cheated on her in a recent trip to Brazil. He had then asked for a divorce. She worked at Cal State Northridge, running a faculty computer lab.

They avoided the ski club that night by going to their own restaurant and making out in the woods behind the condo. They couldn't do more than that as they each had single bunk beds in the condos the group had rented.

He invited her to his home later that week, and they made love in the same bed he had shared with Arabella. Tatiana was a great lover, rather vocal in her expressions, his name coming out, "Nee-store, oh, Nee-store," her skin becoming damp and flushed during love-making. Arabella had never in his memory broken a sweat or said anything while they had made love. For Arabella, love-making must have been just a responsibility. Why hadn't Nestor noticed that before?

Nestor didn't return to Ellington International. He was set. Rosemary, however, felt he was going too fast, and Nestor should date others at the same time.

"But we're making love. I can't see someone else while I do that."

"Why not?"

"My emotions don't work that way. I can only be physically involved with one person at a time. I would think she expects that. When did morals change? It's okay to cheat?"

"It's not cheating, but I'm fine with your approach. Just remember, this isn't about sealing the deal. Don't make big plans, picturing your wedding or whatever."

"Neither one of us is officially divorced, so we're not racing ahead. We just have fun together." Although Nestor and Arabella had signed divorce papers, a judge still had to approve everything.

The next two months were an incredible high for him. His only doubts about if they were truly right for each other was that all her friends were foreign nationals—a lot of Russians as well as South Americans. He was referred to as the "gringo" by some of her friends. Los Angeles seemed quite different when he was with these people.

One evening Tatiana knocked on his door unexpectedly. They hadn't planned to see each other until the next night. She was crying, her whole body posture bent as she hugged herself.

"What's wrong, what's wrong?" he said, pulling her inside and hugging her. She held on as if she'd been pulled from fiery wreckage.

"Alejandro came to my apartment tonight." That was her husband.

"Did he hit you?" Nestor said, ready to fight him, not knowing much about him other than he was shorter.

"No," she said meekly, and she looked up. "He apologized for everything, including other things over the years, things I'd always wanted him to say. He said he loved me, and he was the stupidest man in the world for wanting a divorce. He pleaded to let him back in. Our children showed up, too, and pleaded along with their father. He really is a different man. So, you know...."

"What did you say?"

"I said yes. I can't see you anymore. I'm sorry, Nestor, my dear lovely man. You are an amazing person, and I hate to lose you, but I must." She gave him one last, impassioned kiss, then turned and left, leaving him speechless. Once he heard her car start, he ran out. As she backed her black Honda SUV out of his driveway, he waved good-bye.

Bye.

Shit, shit, shit, shit, shit. Inside something gave way, like a jet with no engines, gliding for a crash. Why was this happening to him? He hadn't been ready to commit, but still he'd thought he and Tatiana were an item. How much heartbreak could his heart take? He found himself walking down his street in the dark, listening to a dog bark, then the sad sound of a violin from another house. Why did Alejandro come back? Why why why?

A showrunner friend of his at Warners, an African-American man his age named Zheek but who preferred to be called "Z," met him in the commissary for their nearly weekly lunches. A thin fellow who always wore black clothes with a beret, Z produced a sitcom called, *The Secrets of Love*, which took place in a gentrifying Bronx neighborhood with a rising but quirky black family. There was a wise but quipping dad.

"Nestor, buddy, you seem so down. No sex lately?" Z clapped his back.

"Maybe never again," said Nestor, who went on to explain how Tatiana left.

"Tatiana, she was the one, right? Oh, this is bad news," said Z, who put his head in his hands.

"You look as bad now as I do."

"I'm a married guy, and very happy, but I live for your exploits. It gives me a chance to dream."

"No more dreamin'," said Nestor. "You might like hearing what I go through, but it isn't particularly easy to live it."

Z laughed. "I have to remember that line. You sometimes inspire my show, you know. I used that scene of you meeting Tatiana on a ski slope. I put in on Gore Mountain near New York. People loved it!"

"Black people skiing?"

"Yeah, and we swim, too!"

When Nestor next saw Rosemary, she said, "I'm sorry about what happened, but you've been open to living, open to the moment, and that's a good thing. This is just part of the path."

He nodded. He didn't know what to say or what his path might be, other than it was paved with good intentions.

Without asking, Rosemary made him mint tea from her hot plate and handed it to him. He rather liked it, and he just sipped. Mint. He should have more mint in his life.

She smiled softly at him. "Buddha said, 'No one saves us but ourselves. No one can and no one may. We ourselves must walk the path."

This is why he came to see her. He couldn't ever think of these things. It was good to have an advisor. She advised him to take a week off, then get back to dating. A week later, he returned to Ellington.

Number 11 was a woman who had left him five messages in the two months he had been away from Ellington. She was in real estate, and she skied and scuba-dived. She commented highly on his skiing pictures and said she was looking for companionship with a skier.

He contacted her, saying he hadn't noticed her emails until now and profusely apologized. He said he loved skiing and said if she wanted to talk, call him, and he gave his phone number. That led to a first date at a jazz club, where they ate steak and danced the night away. They had a second date bowling. He learned she'd been di-

vorced for eighteen years but had two significant relationships after that.

She suggested an art walk downtown, but then a day
later, she sent an email that her boyfriend of many years
had cheated on her just two months ago, and she'd left
him. She thought she was over him but realized she
wasn't. She sounded much like Sharon over her loss.
Why was online dating so hard? he asked himself. He
was the guy in the silent movie shorts who always slipped
on the banana.

He wrote Number 11 back that he'd enjoyed meeting
her. Goodbye and good luck.

The next person he wrote happened after he'd been
mesmerized by a picture of her in skis at the top of
Mammoth. Maybe he'd find another Tatiana. Her eyes
seemed so honest, too. He wrote her immediately, men-
tioning his love of skiing, and within minutes, she wrote
back, "Nestor? I thought you said your wife came back to
you? Remember how we met at the Beachwood Café?" It
was Milena again.

He wrote to Milena, "Whoops." Should he say more?
A *whoops* alone would be callous, but did she really need
to know more? He added, "My wife left again, and you
have new pictures. I didn't recognize you. The new pictures flatter you. We don't match, though. Sorry."

That day, he made a list of the women he'd met and
their names. He didn't want this mistake to occur again.
Never in his life had he met so many women. Was he
learning anything? Yes. He accepted humiliation like a
gold watch.

The next and real Number 12, another real estate
agent, kept chattering about how the last guy she saw, a
married general, flew her all over America but returned
to his wife. Gregarious, she wore expensive rings and a
gold necklace.

Number 13, whom he met the same week, was similar, talking about her former lover, a *Los Angeles Times* sports columnist who had swept her off to Super Bowls and soccer tournaments in Hawaii. Nestor couldn't keep up with those standards and saw them each only once.

Number 14 was an actress who said she'd done big things on TV, but when they met in person, he couldn't stand her high voice. When he looked her up on IMDB, he found she had such roles as "girl at bar" on *CSI* and "girl waiting for bus" on a *Law and Order* episode. Did that qualify her as professional? If he were an actor, his role would be "man flailing and drowning in river."

Number 15 was the CEO of a children's clothing company down in the fashion district, a blonde named Carly who had just turned fifty. He didn't ask if she knew Sharon. Carly suggested sushi for lunch in Pasadena, across from a big black building that had a huge orange dot outside of the top floor and the words "Art Center" on it. Pasadena was slightly out of his zone, but by expanding his radius, he had more choices.

At the restaurant, dressed well and braless, Carly pointed out her new Jaguar in the lot. As she spoke with a big husky laugh at times, she'd touch his arm. Was she seducing him? When they left, he swore she was expecting a kiss, but on a first date at lunch?

The second date with her was at Mike and Ann's, an elegant South Pasadena restaurant where he ate great short ribs. Afterward, she asked if he'd like to go whiskey tasting. He didn't like whiskey, but he should stay open to the moment, right? She grabbed him by the hand, and they simply walked to another bar down the street and ordered a flight. Next thing he knew, they were at her condo nearby, yanking off their clothes. When she asked for a condom—he hadn't expected this to happen—he didn't have one. Heck, he had never had one. She rummaged in her bathroom and found one. His penis seemed willing, so he put it on. She dove into him as if he were a pool. Her skin dampened quickly. She was a screamer. He never knew a woman to scream happily while making love. Maybe it was the whiskey.

Afterward, she said he could find his way out of her house. The door would lock automatically. On the sidewalk walking toward the restaurant and his car, he felt as if he were back in high school. The sex hadn't been bad. She must be into him, he reasoned. It seemed quick for a meaningful relationship, but maybe she was simply ready for one.

After a few more dates, always a week apart, always at her place, he noticed she had two extra bedrooms that appeared high schoolish and feminine.

"Do you have daughters?"

"Yes. When I see you, they're with their dad."

She nuzzled his neck. He rubbed her back. She kissed him hard. No time for talking now. He expected they'd chat about their kids at some point, maybe after sex. She always was so amorous when he came over, eager to pull him into bed. He'd never thought of himself as a stud. Maybe he was a stud. If so, why did he feel confused?

Later, after making love, he asked, "Are we boyfriend and girlfriend?"

She gasped and said, "Why do guys always want a girlfriend? Why can't we just have fun?"

"This is a fling? It feels meaningful to me. I could hug you all night while watching TV."

"I share two daughters with my ex, who's a cop. When they're with him," she said, "I see you one night." *A cop? With a gun?* But he said nothing.

He stared at himself in the mirror above the bed. He'd never noticed the mirror before.

"How many nights a week do you have off?" he asked.

"Three. I have one for you."

Was she was seeing other guys, too?

He said, "Am I in a different universe?"

"I can't do the wifey shit anymore, worrying if tonight was the night my husband would get shot to death."

"I never get shot."

"I'm too busy running a company for monogamy shit," she said.

That was that.

In the morning, he awoke with a sense of hopelessness. He was Sisyphus, pushing the dating bolder forever up the hill.

In the years he'd been married, had people forgotten how to connect? Carly was like his son Josh, no time for a romantic relationship. Was Nestor on an impossible quest for connection? These days, maybe everyone loved his or her smartphones so much, perhaps that's all they needed. The future was now.

Nestor took two weeks off, then hit Ellington International once again.

Number 16 was an executive chef for hire by rich people. She apparently did well, had a staff of five, and was far heavier than her pictures—probably a downside to her profession. He took her to a great French restaurant, knowing she was a chef. She had seemed so funny on the phone but was less so in person. She simply talked quickly and nonstop. He could hardly get a word in. Chemistry was everything, right?

They hugged at her Hummer, and he knew he'd never hear from her again. He didn't contact her, either. That seemed to be standard for online dating: contact could simply cease, no explanation or thank-you's.

Date Number 17 came from an Ellington-sponsored Meet-N-Greet at the Getty Museum. As he stepped off the Getty's shuttle train that brought him from the bottom of the mini-mountain to the top, he saw a sign that said, "Ellington Singles," with an arrow pointing to an area by the stairs. The stairs led to the galleries and gardens, Valhalla on a hill. From a distance, he could see about a dozen people gathered.

One of two women with Ellington name tags checked him in and said, "Welcome. Just stand or sit over there, and we'll start in about ten minutes."

The men were gathered on one side, a few talking to each other in folding chairs, and the women were away from them, chatting with each other. Nestor returned to the table and said, "I'm sorry. Am I supposed to sit a-mong all the men?"

The woman laughed. "This happens all the time. It's supposed to be a mixer, and I swear it's like junior high dances, each side a stranger to the other. Don't worry. We'll mix it up."

As he looked at all the women, most seemed older than him—elegant, but somewhere in their sixties or seventies. Two, though, one blonde, one redhead, seemed to be in their forties. Both were focused, however, on a Greek-God-looking man in his fifties, longish gray hair and a black T-shirt. Over that, he wore a blue blazer, like the Dos Equis guy from the Most Interesting Man in the World commercials.

"Do you like art?" said the blonde to the man.

"Not particularly," he said. "Just moved here from San Francisco."

"What part of town are you in?" said the blonde.

"Pasadena."

"Pasadena!" said the redhead. "The Pasadena Play-house is great! Do you like theatre?"

"Not particularly," he said. He seemed to have more interesting things to do in his mind as he looked at the upscale homes in the hills across the freeway. Perhaps he thought he could see filmmaker Stephen Spielberg's house. The Most Interesting Man in the World was ready for his close-up.

"I love the theatre," said Nestor without thinking he was barging in. "Did you see Arthur Miller's *A View from the Bridge* at the Ahmanson?"

"Oh!" the redhead said, squeaking with delight. "From a Dutch director, I forgot his name."

"Ivo van Hove," said Nestor. "He's from Belgium, actually, but works in Amsterdam. Wasn't the play amazing with nearly no props?"

"And the actors were barefoot. That production blew me away!"

From that point on, he and the redhead, Niamh, pronounced "Neave," a Celtic name, walked through the galleries together on the tour, chatting with each other. It turned out she wasn't even in Ellington International. Her blonde friend was, and her friend hadn't wanted to go alone. Soon thereafter, he and Niamh ended up going on three dates in short order, two of them to plays. Nestor liked her, but she seemed to have a big bubble around her. She stated early on that she didn't like holding hands. Maybe she just had a warm-up period, and later she'd like touching—or maybe she was still reeling from her divorce. He couldn't understand, but he was trying to be patient and live in the here and now with her.

On the positive side, she loved talking about theatre as did he. He discovered she had been living in Italy for the last twenty years, married to an Italian, until two years ago when her daughter went off to college in England, and she decided to live with her daughter and divorce her husband.

"Why did you divorce?" asked Nestor on the third date.

"Well, no reason really," she said. "I just didn't want to be married. It didn't feel right. He was a nice guy, I'll say that. He was just so, I don't know: Italian."

Nestor didn't see her after that. She was too much like Arabella, he decided. She'd acted on whim rather than talking anything out. He stopped calling.

Was he like Happy Loman in *Death of a Salesman*, never happy, really just yearning for attention? Was midlife love really just that, a quest for the feeling of a long-ago parent showing care and concern?

That night in bed by himself, listening to the repetitive, trance-like melody of *The Photographer* by Philip Glass, he recalled how Arabella detested Glass's music. She called it a nightmare, a rat running on an endless wheel. Maybe that's what online dating was.

No, the dates might seem similar, but each one was different and pleasant enough at the time. Not one of them was a nightmare. He would now tell Arabella if you listened closely to Philip Glass compositions, the rhythm and music weren't mere minimalism, caught in a cycle, but were building toward something meaningful, a burst of wonder. The female vocalists in this piece, even if they uttered simple sounds, buoyed him.

Number 18 was Kotta, pronounced "Coda." He tried to remember the pronunciation as the last syllable in "South Dakota." She lived in Santa Monica by the beach— normally out of his preferred radius, but what the hell. She suggested breakfast at the beach—how wonderful! Maybe they'd walk on the sand afterward. When he arrived, she was the only one there, but she looked nothing like her photos online. Then he saw the resemblance. Maybe her images had been from happier times. Now she looked worn out and sad. When he ordered Eggs Benedict with extra lemon for the hollandaise sauce, she burst out crying, saying that's exactly what her ex-husband would have ordered, the bastard.

Number 19 said she really wasn't divorced but was a widow. She felt that "widow" wouldn't appeal to men, so she chose "divorced" for the website.

"It sounds better, don't you think?" she asked.

Was one loss better than another? "Have you dated in seven years?" he asked.

"No, but my three grown kids, two boys and a girl, urged me to date. Then I realized, I'm getting older. I need someone to help me when I get old." She smiled shyly, as if getting older was something she only just discovered, like learning there's caffeine in Coke. "What if I get dementia?" she asked.

And what would I have to feed you? he wondered. *Mashed yeast?*

"In seven years..." Nestor said, still thinking how to frame his question. "In seven years, have you missed, you know, the act of lovemaking?"

"Sex?" she said. "Haven't missed it. At our ages, what's the point, right?"

He scratched her name out in his mind. He also wondered if it would take Sharon seven years to date again.

Number 20 was a post-production person at Netflix and only wanted to meet at a coffee shop. She was well-coifed, with clipped speech, and at the end said, "I don't feel a romantic connection. There's no spark. Bye." She shook his hand.

Number 21, a paralegal specializing in divorce, totally dour, at some point admitted she wasn't actually divorced because she never married. She didn't like marriage. She said, "I see divorce on a daily basis. Is anyone really happy?"

Later, over cheesecake, she said she never moved in with her boyfriend but was more like his sex slave. She'd felt like those teenagers in Detroit held in chains for sex. "Except I'm fifty-four." She ended the night by saying, "Our lives are all over anyway, right? We're just waiting for death."

Many women, he realized, seemed to think if they went through the motions of dating, they'd find a mysterious something, like phlogiston, which would carry them to new highs. Phlogiston, as he'd learned in high school science, had been an imagined and invisible element given off in burning. Wood was guessed to be ash and phlogiston. To him, intimacy was tangible, not mysterious. It was oxygen and much more than sex. It was holding hands and laughing together. What happened to holding hands and laughing together?

Number 22 was a breath of fresh air, a nurse practitioner named Marybeth who had reached out to him. She lived in South Pasadena, a place he knew little about, aside from Mike and Ann's and his date with Carly. It wasn't Pasadena but, yes, south of it, a place known for its good schools. She suggested they meet at Mike and Ann's. Was that the only restaurant there? It would be his birthday, but he had nothing else going on that day. He asked if he could pick her up. That's the way he'd done it in high school, when there had been clearer lines within dating. She said sure.

She lived at the top of the tallest hill with a breathtaking view of South Pasadena, El Sereno, and downtown Los Angeles. As he gazed at the view, standing next to her rose garden, her front door opened, and she stepped out.

"You must be Nestor," she said with delight, auburn hair circling her cheerful face. "I'm Marybeth."

"You look as great as your pictures." He turned toward her, and they kissed each other's cheeks. "And what a view you have here!" he said.

"When I bought this house after the divorce," Marybeth said, "it was just one bedroom, one bath. I expanded it for my two kids. They're adults now. A boy and a girl."

He liked her right away, the way she looked at him with interest when he spoke, the way she laughed easily. As he drove with her to Mike and Ann's, she spoke about how her mother had called that day. "She lives in Buffalo, New York. Ever been there?"

"No, but in the winter, it's in the news often for its snowstorms."

"Lots of snow," she said. "Why my mother stays there, I don't know. She said she'll never move. I worry about her."

"Doesn't she love your house on the hill?"

"She says L.A. is just too crowded. I told her, it just takes one fall on an icy sidewalk to break a hip. Aging parents. Are yours alive?"

"Alas, no," he said. "I was orphaned when I hit sixty."

She laughed. "You're right. We all become orphans."

Marybeth seemed unarmed like Annie in *Annie Hall*. Once they were at a charming outdoor table at the restaurant, she asked, "What's your astrological sign?

"Leo," he said. "In fact, today is my birthday, and I'm taking you out."

"I'm buying you dinner!" she blurted, happy, and took his hand. "And I'm a Gemini—very compatible!"

"No, please let me pay because you are my present," he said. She smiled. They had a fabulous dinner.

When Marybeth went to the bathroom, he noticed a familiar face—Carly's, the whisky-tasting woman. She was rubbing the arm of a suave, gray-haired man—the same guy he'd seen at the Getty, the Most Interesting Man in the World. This was too bizarre. God had fun with his people, it seemed. Carly and the Most Interesting Man recognized him, pointed at him, waved, and then got back to each other. She'd be screaming in delight that night.

Marybeth returned just then and said, "You know them? I thought South Pasadena was new to you?"

"Film people," he said. "Life is funny, no?" When he asked the waiter for the bill, the young man said, "The lady has already paid."

"Happy birthday," Marybeth said with a big smile.

Nestor was eager to see her again, and they set it through email for the weekend. He said he'd take her to a cooking class he found in Santa Monica, focused on pastry and bread dough because she'd told him she wished she knew how to make bread. She was ecstatic. Before the weekend, though, she called, sadness in her voice, to say that her mother in Buffalo needed her help—her mother had broken her hip on the stairs in the summer. Marybeth was flying off the next day. "I'm unlikely to see you again," she said. "I'm likely to stay there a while. Life seems just so odd the way it unfolds." She wished him good luck in dating.

Nestor felt a mixture of sadness and frustration. He and Marybeth had had such promise. Were people just dandelion fluff in the wind of time?

Number 23, Danielle, turned out to be just as friendly and caring. Twenty years younger than he was, he'd written to her on Ellington because she showed a picture of herself sitting among people in a concert. She was cute with a short, fashionable hair style. The caption said she and her brother saw David Gilmour at the Hollywood Bowl in January.

He had been to that concert—both nights, actually. Gilmour was from Pink Floyd, and anyone who loved Pink Floyd had to be great. They emailed back and forth a few times, and when they talked on the phone, he loved her easy laugh. He said he'd like to take her to dinner. She agreed. And what food did she love? Sushi, so they met at a sushi place in Hollywood.

When she walked in, he waved to her from the sushi bar, saving her a place. She walked with a glow and a smile, as if they knew each other already. He stood and shook her hand, and then she kissed his cheek. She was shorter than he was at around five-foot-three.

The sushi bar, oval-shaped, had little sailboats that floated in a circle. Each boat held a plate of sushi—either rolls, such as Rainbow, Dragon, and California Rolls, or pieces of raw fish such as salmon or halibut on a band of white rice. The idea was to grab the sushi you liked and eat it. You'd pay by the plate later.

Sushi told a lot about a person. If she ate, say, salmon roe, she was adventurous. If she ate nothing raw—only cooked egg or cooked shrimp—then she was not ready for change. Danielle went for the salmon roe right away. He ate a raw quail egg.

"You said in your profile," he began, "that you have a green card, but I hear you don't speak with any sort of accent."

"My mother is from El Salvador, where there was a civil war going on in the eighties. She'd been raped at fifteen by a national soldier and fled to America with her parents. I was the product of that rape."

"Raped? Jeez."

"At sixteen, my mom took up with a long-distance truck driver from Amsterdam. Her parents let her marry him at sixteen, and she had my brother two years later. Her husband died in a truck accident shortly after that, so I never really got to know him. And you? Where are you from?"

It took him a few moments to answer after hearing all that. "I'm from here, Los Angeles. My dad was a lawyer and Mom was an astrophysicist at the Jet Propulsion Lab."

"Are they alive?"

"Alas, both have passed from this earth."

"You're very different from me," she said. That's what fascinated him about her. He asked more about her mother. She said, "Mom married another trucker, but

Mom died from pneumonia when I was sixteen. My step-father abandoned my brother and me, just drove his big truck out one day, never to be seen again."

"Such traumas in your life," said Nestor, amazed. "How do you have such a good attitude?"

"I've never felt like a sufferer," she said. "I steer my life. After my stepdad moved out, I managed to pay the rent for two years with the little my mother left us and by working after school. I raised my brother."

"What job?"

"I was a barista. When I graduated high school in Whittier, I agreed to marry my high-school sweetheart if my brother was part of the package."

He looked at her with amazement. "How old were you?"

"Eighteen. We married. After the birth of our daughter, my husband really got into heroin. He overdosed and died."

"Yikes," he said.

She kissed him spontaneously as raw fish swirled around them.

After they made love two dates later, they dated exclusively, and she always insisted on coming to his house, where they made love almost every date. She could slink out of her clothes like a salamander with its skin. She'd laugh in anticipation. She insisted on condoms as she wasn't using birth control.

He took her out to dinner often, just so it didn't seem as if it were all about sex. She seemed to crave lovemaking but she was different from Carly. Danielle moved more slowly and tenderly. Danielle never spent the night. She lived with her brother still, so they couldn't go to her place. Her brother, he learned, had an incident working at a tire store. When he was repairing a tire one day, it exploded, and the steel wheel hit his head, leaving him with the intelligence of an eight-year-old. She would probably care for him the rest of her life.

She'd met Nestor's friends at an afternoon barbecue he gave one Saturday. Polite, she nonetheless came off as standoffish, even to him. At first, she sat at a different table from his, until he insisted she sit with him. She asked why? He said she was breaking up another couple by sitting where she was. She was just so different from when he was alone with her. He realized that although he had heard about her coworkers, her daughter, her grandson, her brother, and her friends, he had never met any of them.

One evening, as her car drove off, he hopped into his black Kia and followed her at a distance, the way detectives did in cop shows. In the flats of Hollywood, she parked on the street and walked into a bungalow-style apartment complex built around a small garden and fountain, like the San Bernadino Arms right out of the 1975 movie *The Day of the Locust,* with Donald Sutherland and Karen Black. It was stucco with arched doorways and windows. He saw her walk into one apartment.

The next morning when she went to work, Nestor returned to her place to see if he could grab a view of her brother. He saw an Amazon truck drop something right on their doorstep, and the driver pushed the doorbell. As the driver walked off, Nestor hurried over and picked up the package. It was addressed to a man named Phillip Sestina. He assumed it was Danielle's invalid brother. When the door opened, Nestor said to the tall, savvy-looking man, "Are you Phillip?"

"Yes, I am." Nestor handed him the package. The guy didn't look incapacitated in any way. "I love this little complex," Nestor said.

"It's a shoebox of an apartment, but we're both actors, so it's nice," said the man.

"I only delivered here once before—to someone named Danielle."

"My wife," said Phillip.

"Have a good day," said Nestor.

The next time Danielle called, Nestor said, "Who is Phillip? Your brother?"

There was a long pause. "I can see you're nosy. That's too bad. You'll never see me or hear from me again. I won't answer your phone calls, email, or texts. Stay away. Have a good life, Nestor." She hung up.

While he had the urge to call her right back and ask "Why?" and many other questions, he did not. He didn't ever try to communicate with her again as he couldn't imagine how someone so friendly could lie like that. What was she after? Not love. Was it his money? At one point, she had mentioned she loved diamonds, showing off a ring she'd bought for herself that she wore on her index finger. Another time, she mentioned her birthday was coming up. In fact, it was supposed to be in a week. He'd already bought her a diamond necklace, very expensive.

He tried to fathom how she could have toyed with his emotions, overpower him even? She—or she and her husband—saw him as an acting challenge? Or was it just about money? This made him consider his own faults. Did he want a relationship so much that he'd pretend he was in one? Had he been in love? Was love just attraction and sex?

He thought he had a relationship with Danielle, but he'd thought the same thing with Arabella. Maybe he didn't know love at all. No, he loved his son. He had loved Arabella. He'd been on the verge of loving Tatiana the skier, and then Danielle, but he knew, honestly, he hadn't fully believed either was love. Love, he knew, was a powerful feeling but over a lot of time. It was also about trusting yourself it was love. Maybe love could be an equation, like Einstein's equation E=mc². Love, he decided, was connective energy multiplied by time squared plus trust: L = et²+T. That helped him for about two minutes. Otherwise, he felt black inside.

He'd lay in bed in the mornings, inert as a cucumber.

I just can't do this anymore. It hurts. His relationship with Danielle had hurt perhaps as deeply as Arabella leaving him. He spoke with Arabella once in a while, and they were friendly again, especially when it came to their son. Arabella had been real. Danielle hadn't.

Dating was a bizarre entertainment, he decided, akin to sky diving or ski jumping. We were all just falling. In fact, he started wondering how any two people on Earth stayed married. Everyone had such different needs, outlooks, motivations, and personalities. Perhaps we were all alone.

He felt like punching God.

"Stay present in the moment," Rosemary reminded him again at their next meeting. Yes, he must.

He didn't have the heart to return to Ellington. This was it. He was destined to live alone, maybe become a cat guy, live with dozens of cats and call them cute names like Mrs. Minniver and Judy Sprinkles. Maybe he could become the old guy of the neighborhood who would yell at the kids on skateboards to slow down or they'll break their necks. He'd replace Mr. James down the street, who had passed away last year, leaving his dog, Shadow.

If only he could have met someone else like Sharon, the widow. She had been more than twenty women and six months ago. He wondered if she'd started dating again and if her business was doing okay.

His curiosity got the best of him. Before he censored himself, he sent Sharon an email, one that said, "I've been thinking of you and all life's thrown at you—and me. I struggle to understand loss myself. Just know you left an impression on me. You're a good person. Keep being good." He ended with a smiley emoji and his name and sent it.

He didn't expect to get a reply, and he didn't for three days.

Then he saw her name at the top of his email list. She wrote, "Nestor, you're someone I never expected to hear from again. I've thought of you, too, and how nice you were, but I just wasn't ready then. My daughter, though, gained her license, and I bought her a car. Now I hardly ever see her, alas.

"Still, the independence has made her more assured, optimistic even. It's been hard to let my birdy get her flying wings. You did it with your son, so you know. We're off to Hawaii tomorrow for a short vacation, so thank you for your kind note. May you be well."

She signed it, "Fondly, Sharon."

Fondly, he thought. *That's positive.* Nothing else about the note said, "Write me again," but he did, anyway. All he wrote was, "Enjoy Hawaii. Send me a picture."

A week later, she sent him three pictures, of palm trees, ocean, and amazing skies of clouds and sunsets.

Over the next month, their emails grew in length and regularity. They set up a time to talk on the phone, and when they did, she told him about her job, working with clothing designers and manufacturers. With a great sales team, she was making a steady profit.

She asked more about what he did. He told her about producing an animated show and pushing the writers and convincing the studio to approve his stories. He worked with amazing directors, animators, and voice talent. Then of course, there's the marketing department to get people to see their work on the Cartoon Network. ComicCon in San Diego each summer was a big event for him.

They met for dinner at a Los Feliz diner, Fred 62. They both ordered a veggie burger and white wine, and he asked about where her daughter went to high school.

"Vivie's a junior at Immaculate Heart, a school for girls. It's important for girls to get a separate education. Girls get so easily overshadowed by boys in high school."

"My mother felt the same way," said Nestor. "My two older sisters went to girls' schools. Unfortunately, I went to an all-boys school, which probably's the reason it's taken me so long to understand women. My two ex-wives probably can attest to that."

"You're a good listener," she said. "Not all guys are."

"Believe me, I love our conversation."

"Are you free next Saturday for a movie?" she asked him.

He was about to say "absolutely" when he realized he had a party to go to—his own party at his house. A month ago, he'd decided that being single didn't mean he couldn't celebrate. "Come to my house," he told Sharon. "I'm having a party." She accepted.

When she arrived, she was not shy but spoke easily with the ten people there. Perhaps her job in talking to strangers every day helped. His friends grinned and whispered in his ear. "Are you dating her?" Each time he said, "No, we're just friends."

Sharon sat next to him at dinner—nothing awkward as with Danielle. At the end of the night, after he'd walked Sharon to her car and shook her hand good-night, he returned to his party, which was abuzz. "How did you meet her?" people asked.

He didn't want to get into the whole online dating thing or his and Sharon's history, so he said, "Through other friends. We're not dating."

One woman, deeply in love with Nestor's doctor friend, said, "If you're not dating her, I will!" Everyone laughed.

At his next appointment, Rosemary asked him if he was on Ellington again. No, he wasn't ready, but perhaps soon. He had mentioned previously his contacting Sharon, and now he admitted to seeing her. Rosemary smiled and sat forward like Z, wanting to hear the latest twists.

"Nothing big," said Nestor. "We're not even talking about dating. Best I can tell, we're friends. Of everyone I've seen, though, she stands out."

"People who've lost spouses are different. You have to act within her personal time frame."

"She's not ready for dating. I'm not acting as a partner-wanted ad. We just like each other."

"What makes her different from the others?"

He smiled. "She's unpretentious. She is both vulnerable and strong. I feel alive when I'm with her."

"Thinking about the others you've dated, what have you learned from them?"

He laughed. "More patience. I tamp down expectations. Despite my less-than-amazing experiences, I'm a damn optimist. There's someone for everyone, maybe even me."

"Beautiful," she said. "I wish all my clients were as positive as you."

When he left that day, Rosemary gave him a hug.

Sharon called and asked if he'd like to come over for dinner at her place, to reciprocate for his party.

"Dinner at *your* place?" He whistled.

"It's not a big deal. It's just easier for me with my work schedule. How's this Friday?"

"You're not anxious like you were six months ago?"

"I look at you as a friend. You seem nice. I could use a male friend."

"No problem," he said, hopes partly dashed. "I'm happy to have dinner with you."

Vivie would be working at Sephora that night, she said, which is why Sharon could have dinner with him.

"Vivie would not want to see her mother with another man," said Sharon.

After they hung up, he sighed. *She's a good woman but still not ready for romance.*

Sharon and Vivie lived in Los Feliz, not far from him. On the way over, he reminded himself that the second he suggested romantic interest, she might call it off again. He could be a friend. It was nice not to have expectations, actually. It wasn't the Yes/No of the usual dating.

Sharon's house featured a gated courtyard framed by white walls and shaded by a giant magnolia tree in the center. The house, with its skylights and wood floors, felt friendly, with two landscape paintings on one wall and a tasteful arrangement of framed photos on another. In every photo stood a tall round-faced man with Sharon or with Vivie. In the shots, Vivie ranged in age from baby to middle-school. Sharon looked steadily gorgeous in each one, as if she didn't age. The man went from thin to heavy. "Sorry about so many Frank photos, but it helps my daughter."

"It's nice he loved you both so much," said Nestor. "To feel that... That's what we all want, right?"

She looked at him more closely and smiled.

The doorbell rang. "It's dinner," said Sharon. She had ordered from a restaurant down the street, and UberEats was delivering it.

Nestor found the salmon, fingerling potatoes, and green beans with béarnaise sauce hot and delicious. They got to talking about music at one point. "Do you like concerts?" she said. "Not that I know of any coming up."

"I saw Coldplay at the Rose Bowl with my son in the last year or so."

"Coldplay! They played twice at the Rose Bowl on their *Head Full of Dreams* Tour. Their first concert was the last concert Frank and I attended before he died."

"Frank and I have similar tastes, clearly."

"Vivie and I went to the second concert after Frank's passing." She paused, then said, "I still miss him. Frank was a really great guy—as you are. I hope you don't mind I brought him up yet again."

"He's a part of your past. You can't fence off your history, particularly the good stuff. I feel the same way about Arabella. We had two great decades. I don't hate her. She's part of my past. So is my job."

She asked him more about the Green Lantern, the star of his animated series, as they stepped to the couch for an HBO movie she'd suggested. He explained there have been several superheroes appearing as the Green Lantern over the years in DC Comics and films. His series revolved around Hal Jordan, a loose cannon of a Green Lantern guy, not unlike Mel Gibson's character in the *Lethal Weapon* series, but this takes place on earth and outer space. Hal Jordan has his motto: "In brightest day, in blackest night, no evil shall escape my sight."

She laughed and said they should see a movie together, a superhero one, the latest in the *Spiderman* series. *Should I read into that?* he wondered.

The next thing he knew, she was moving in for a kiss. *Am I reading this wrongly?* No, she definitely was kissing him, and he was kissing back, there beneath the wall of photos.

A few days later, after he and Sharon had zipped off to the Chinese Theater in Hollywood, he pondered superheroes during the movie. Superheroes were exaggerated, but they were what we wanted in humanity—not someone manipulating you, but someone quietly watching out for you, someone who had true empathy. Surely, good people must exist.

He glanced at Sharon as she turned her head toward him. She kissed him on the cheek—simple, true, and lovely. He kissed her on the lips. They made out. He hadn't done this in a movie theater since high school.

Afterward, as he and Sharon walked out of the Chinese Theater hand-in-hand and onto Hollywood Boulevard, Darth Vader approached. Rather, a man in a Darth Vader costume clanked up to them. He faced Nestor and said, "The ability to destroy a planet is insignificant next to the power of the Force."

Nestor looked the man right into the eye sockets of his plastic mask and replied, "Be mindful of your thoughts, Anakin. They betray you."

"Oh, my God," cried Sharon. "You're a *Star Wars* fan!" She laughed and grabbed Nestor's other hand, caressing his hands with her thumbs. He smiled because the quote from Obi-Wan Kenobi had popped into his head and reminded him of something Rosemary might say. To him, it meant stripping himself of preconceived notions. It was as if, well, the Force brought him here.

He kissed Sharon's hands in return. They laughed together. The Force was with them.

A Warm Front Appears to be Moving from California and Deep into Minnesota

T he boom came like a jet plane crashing into the woods, slamming into the windowpanes, shaking the room, which made Summer, all five-foot-three of her, jerk up in bed.

Heart pounding, she expected to see the earth cracking open outside of her California ranch house rental. The bed, the bookshelves, and the bureau, however, all stood firmly. A flash of lightning now startled her anew, and she remembered she was in Minnesota in her parents' house, not in California with her boyfriend, and outside was a Midwestern rainstorm. The thunder echoed back from the trees, and the rain hammered like dropped marbles on the roof. It made her laugh—she was so happy it was just a storm, not an earthquake.

Now energized, she leaped out of bed, shucked her nightshirt, and put on fresh panties when her mother entered. Summer covered her breasts and yelled "Mom!"

"I've seen those before. Glad to see ya inherited my genes," said her mother in her Scottish accent.

Summer put on the bra she'd worn the day before. She looked at her mother. "I'm assuming you didn't come in here to tell me something about my breasts." Summer aimed herself at the black pants and black T-shirt in her suitcase.

"I thought I heard you cryin'," said her mother.

"I was laughing."

"Oh?" Her face brightened. "That's different, then." She sat on the bed. "School's startin' again for me in a few days," said Summer's mother. "Summer's over."

"You told me that last night." Her mother was an accountant for the cafeteria at Deephaven Elementary School and had the summers off—very different from her earlier life as a top fashion model in Scotland and England. That's when she'd met drummer Kyle Green, Summer's real dad, of the famous progressive rock band Johnson, Johns, and Green. He was a legend known for his aggressive drumming and his pranks.

"If you're worried what I'll do while you're at work, I don't need taking care of," said Summer. "I'm going to look for an apartment today in Dinkytown."

"Can't you find something closer?"

"In the stupid suburbs? No, and besides, Reed's hoping to transfer to 'Em-cad'."

"What the hell's that?"

"Minneapolis College of Art and Design. They have a good film program. Still, I thought we'd live near the U for the energy." The "U" was the University of Minnesota.

"You have money for that?" her mother said.

"Yeah. My royalty check came." Her real father had OD'd when she was three, so his estate and royalty checks had gone to her, his only child, and included his Malibu house and his English castle, which had racked up a lot of debt. It'd taken years for accountants to figure it out, and then her mother had burned through much of the rest in big houses, nannies for Summer, and trips and parties for herself—until Summer turned eighteen. Because the remaining band was still kickass—even if they were a geezer band—she earned money on the older albums.

"If ya had money, why didn't you stay out in California?" said her mother.

"All my friends are here—as are you and Dad." Her stepfather was "Dad," and after things were so messed up when Summer was twelve, he'd moved them to Minnesota for a normal life.

"Besides," said Summer. "Reed needs to concentrate on his latest film."

"Now what if, dear... I mean, just suppose Reed doesn't come?"

"Why do you have to be so negative? You're always like a vampire, sucking out my happiness."

"Are you still sober?" said her mother.

"Are you? Jeez, why do you have to ask that?"

"Because we both have this extra challenge."

"I suppose you turning me into your drinking buddy when I was eleven had nothing to do with my condition?"

"Water under the bridge."

"Gin under the bridge!"

"And so you run off for a filmmaker in California?"

"You ran off with Kyle!"

Her mother looked away as if to calm herself down—or perhaps hide the hurt. She stood. "Reed is poorer and has no future—and he loves California from what ya said. Does he really want ta move where the weather's miserable and gray half the year?"

"Love isn't about weather!"

"Honey, ya need ta open your eyes."

Summer was about to blurt, "You're going to tell me how to live life, expert that you are?" but she knew they'd yell at each other and Summer would blame her once again for having had wild parties where Mom's musician friends would fondle her when Mom wasn't in sight.

As if Mom heard her thoughts, Mom said, "I've made some mistakes."

Summer nodded. "Do you know Chagall's painting *Over the Town*?"

"Can't say that I do."

"Sometimes when I'm with Reed, I feel like that painting, carried by my lover and floating, embraced, over a simple town."

"That's nice." Her mother flattened a fold in the blanket as if it mattered.

"I missed this place, you know?" said Summer. "Reed saw that and suggested I move back, and he'd follow after the semester. He loves me."

"Okay," said her mother.

"I'm not little anymore," said Summer. "I've a good sense of what I'm doing. Reed will be an important filmmaker someday. You'll see."

Mom nodded, turned, and padded to her bedroom at the end of the long hall, the other side of the Frank Lloyd Wright Usonian house. The entire length of hallway had wooden cupboards, which stored Mom's English tea sets among other things. The house was known as the crazy house in the neighborhood as it had a towering peak on an otherwise mostly flat roof. There were floor-to-ceiling windows in the living room and dining room, and no basement or attic—not entirely practical in Minnesota's harsh winters.

Summer swept into the kitchen, which was open to the dining room and TV room. She pictured the kind of place she'd rent for Reed and herself. Maybe they'd get an upper floor in one of the boxy houses near the U. Maybe it'd have a clawfoot bathtub, and she'd seduce Reed with a bubble bath. Reed tended to be shy; she was usually the initiator. Maybe a good rubber duck in the tub would be fun.

At the built-in table, as she ate a bowl of Chex, Dad turned into the room, looking surprised.

"I didn't expect you up so soon," he said, his thick Russian eyebrows making a peak like the roof.

"I'm off to find a place to rent."

"So soon? I was hoping to make you pancakes."

"I have to catch a bus."

"I always make you pancakes."

"How about for dinner?" She glanced to the clock on the stove. "If I can finish within five minutes, I can cut through the woods and make the bus at Cowen's Corner."

"In the rain? Let me eat with you, and I'll drive you to the corner."

She nodded.

Dad poured himself Chex, too. "People Chow," he muttered. He ate them, crunching loudly, which she always hated. She didn't broadcast her crunches.

"Your Mom's been telling me about Reed. So why would he want to move to Minnesota? The film industry in Minneapolis isn't exactly bustling."

"And I'm not worth moving for? Nice support, Dad."

"I know how guys work."

"I'm here. Besides, the Coen brothers from Minneapolis are big in film, so if they can do it, so can Reed."

"Don't the Coen brothers live in New York now?"

"They made *Fargo* here, didn't they? Geez. Sometimes you just don't believe in me."

"You'll see when you become a mother yourself. You just want to see your little birdies fly strong, do well. I just want you to have a good future."

"He'll make it here!" said Summer.

"I just want you to really ponder what you want. Life goes too fast. Heck, I was twenty-four like yourself only last year it seems. Now I'm fifty."

"I'm fine."

There was a long pause as if he were thinking. "So, I mean, let's say he comes. Then what?"

"What'd you mean 'then what?' No one plans their life like a trip to Bermuda. You just live—right? Until you die? You have a few jobs until then and some good times."

"What kind of job?"

In California, Summer had stumbled into a job at Litton, where she became office manager for a division making parts for the aerospace industry. They specialized in pieces for inertial navigation systems. "INS tells planes where to go, how to get from Los Angeles to Fiji, for instance," she had told Reed's friends. She would never get something as good in Minnesota, land of 10,000 lakes and as many live bait shops.

"Maybe I'll be a waitress in Dinkytown," she said.

"Not one with a bar, I hope."

"No, Dad. Otherwise, I'll start drinking again and getting fucked by Mom's so-called friends, right?" She didn't mean to bring up her past, but, Christ, what did he want?

"We're all over that. I'm just trying to be smart about this so you don't feel you need to drink again."

"I think you just better take me to the bus."

"Shouldn't you have an Option B in case he doesn't make it out here?"

"I'll get my purse. Let's go."

A huge thump came from the dining room, a sound that made her jump again. It wasn't thunder. The storm was over. Summer saw something moving at the base of one of the dining room picture windows. They both walked to the window. A robin outside flapped on the ground. Someone had left one of the sheer curtains open.

Birds, her parents had discovered after they had moved in, would smash into the huge floor-to-ceiling Thermopanes, not sensing the barrier. Sheer curtains stopped that phenomenon, still allowing for plenty of light. Even so, every so often a bird would bash against the glass where a curtain had been left open.

Dad ran out the dining room door while Summer knelt at the base of the window to look at the bird more closely through the glass. The bird stood on its feet, shaking its head like a boxer fresh from the mat, confused, but ready for more. Before Dad got to it, the bird drew out its wings and flew off, back toward the woods, probably to its family and friends.

"Let's go," she told Dad.

Later, at the bus stop, Summer got out and said, "You don't have to worry about me."

"Really?"

"Really."

Dad nodded and drove off in his Mercedes.

At times it'd been hard living with just one person, Reed, but she had five months to prepare again. Truth was, she'd never had a boyfriend for so long. She felt inept. Still, she'd stayed sober, even now—her ninth year.

Dinkytown, Twin Cities' version of New York's Greenwich Village, was on the north edge of the University of Minnesota, just on the other side of the Mississippi River from Minneapolis. There was nothing dinky about it. As Summer once explained to Reed, the name Dinkytown was like the word "Smuckers"; some things defied explanation. She knew there were many old houses and duplexes shared by university students and professors there, and perhaps somebody had a spare floor. The rental would have to fit their budget, meaning her budget. She'd have to work because the royalty checks were not steady. The only way to find a place was to go ask around and check the student newspaper and bulletin boards.

Summer took the bright yellow bus from Cowen's Corner to downtown, where she switched to another bus on Hennepin Avenue. That bus went over the bridge and to the U and Dinkytown.

"You got a lotta nerve to say you are my friend," sang a grungy banjo player outside the Espresso Royale Caffe. "When I was down, you just stood there grinning.'" Summer recognized the old Bob Dylan tune, but it sounded bad on a banjo. Dylan had gotten his start in Dinkytown, so there were always ersatz Dylans around there the way Vegas had fake Elvises. The banjo player seemed to be fixated on a woman in a black halter-top who was reading *Animal Farm* at a table and not paying attention to him at all. He just didn't get the hint. Some guys don't.

Summer strode down the crowded sidewalk toward her friend Molly's apartment. Molly was going to help her look. The street was thick with cars and the impatient young who honked, late for class. In front of the one- and two-story brick buildings of the commercial district, a swirl of young people pushed past her. Even though she looked no older than they, Summer felt older. Dressed in a skirt with hose, a crisp white blouse, and delicate golden earrings that looked like wind chimes, she was an elegant contrast to those in short shorts, baggy pants, and those few with hair colored indigo or emerald and with corkboard faces tagged with nose rings, eyebrow rings, and piercings around their mouths.

A woman in Lycra leggings emerged from a bookstore with a bearded man in shorts and a gray T-shirt. He pushed a three-wheeled baby carriage that held a pair of twins, less than a year old, both asleep. Reed did not want to talk about having a family, a subject that closed him up. He would try to divert her attention to the television or something out the window. He was so obvious. What did he have against babies? It was only a conversation, after all.

Summer walked on, but as she stepped, a worry scratched at her like a prisoner tunneling from his cell. Why had Reed not called yet? Did he now have doubts? She pulled out her cell phone to see if he'd called. He hadn't, and her battery was nearly depleted. In that moment, she realized to her horror that she had not brought her charger. It was still plugged into the wall in Reed's bedroom. She pushed the button to dial his number. As it was dialing, her phone went dead. That was the last of her energy. Now she'd have to buy a phone card or maybe Molly would let her borrow her phone. Surely he had meant to call.

Reaching the block, Summer looked up to Molly's apartment above the California Suntan Clinic. Summer had never thought until now about how weird it was that the sun was equated with California. Of course, Minnesota's winters were far too gray. Now that she had lived in California, however, there was such thing as too much sun. The sun in Los Angeles always penetrated the space like a nuclear flash that wouldn't stop. You squinted. Besides, the sun had never tanned her Scottish skin but only burned her, so she had covered up as best she could. She'd felt as out of place as an Eskimo in India.

Summer looked at the clinic's main window, which featured a poster of a happy young tan couple in swimsuits and suntanning goggles, appearing like aliens from a newly discovered planet. The man was buff, and the woman had Haagen-Dazs-hard breasts—hmm, implants? The two people looked as real as wax bananas.

On the other side of the glass, Summer noticed a translucent statue—no, it was a hologram—of the same couple. They stood only five inches tall, but they had mass. When Summer moved slightly, she could get a real sense of their bodies in space at different angles, and certainly of the man's wide torso. Summer looked through them to the bored young man at the white desk who was reading a dog-grooming magazine. The hologram, the real/unreal, reminded her of Superman in her stepbrother's comic books that she read as a teenager during family car trips. Superman flew off once to an inaccessible mountain range where, in a cave behind a huge steel door, there was his Fortress of Solitude. In his hideaway, he had exact copies of himself—not unlike this hologram—to send off into the world to take his place while he remained alone to think. Summer could use a clone of herself right now. It could be in California, and she could be here.

She opened the glass door and went up the narrow, carpeted staircase and knocked on the white door at the top. A thin woman with a large grin, stringy blond hair, and blue silk pajamas opened the door and said, "Summer."

"Molly!" Summer hugged her.

Molly hugged back weakly and said, "Come in. Do you drink bourbon?"

"No. No thanks," said Summer, thrown by Molly's question. Who their age drank bourbon—and this time of day?

"School's barely started," said Molly as if hearing Summer's thoughts. "It's still summer."

Molly showed her into a surprisingly elegant living room. Danish modern leather furniture sat among real oak bookshelves filled with books (*The Portable Nietzsche, Fear and Trembling*). She also had a wall unit with glass doors. This wasn't the milk-crate-and-plank interior design she remembered Molly having.

Molly must have noted Summer's reaction because Molly said, "My father died; didn't I tell you? Now I'm an orphan."

"Can you be, at twenty-four?"

"So, I got some money. I decided to buy this furniture and stay in grad school."

"You have a nice place."

"Nice," said Molly without meeting Summer's eyes, walking into the kitchen. Calling from there, Molly said, "If you don't want bourbon, is Diet Coke okay?"

"That's fine," said Summer.

Molly returned, holding out a crystal low-ball glass that had clear ice and the pop.

"Thank you," said Summer.

Molly had a similar glass with a slightly lighter-colored liquid. "Have a seat," said Molly, plopping into a leather chair. "So tell me what the fuck happened in California. You and Reed broke up? Men are bastards. If I had his balls—"

"No, no. We didn't break up."

"He needed 'a little space,' is that it?" she said sardonically.

"He's coming after next semester."

"And you believe that?"

Summer wished she wasn't there. Something had happened to her friend, and this bitter bourbon-drinking clone was left in her place. "I don't think you would have liked L.A. either," said Summer. "The Valley gets to a hundred-and-five in the summer for days on end. There are no basements, no thunderstorms—"

"No Mall of Americas?"

"The place is one endless mall. Strip malls are anchored every block or so with a Beef Bowl or a Jack-in-the-Box."

"Lovely."

"No one mows their own lawns there because immigrant gardeners are so cheap."

"My kinda place," said Molly, pointing to a window. "You should see my back yard—better yet, no. My neighbors are complaining of the tall grass and weeds. Cats like it, though."

"The point is I did not get to know the neighbors or anybody other than Reed."

"So love ain't what it's made out to be?"

"You can't have just one person. My friends are here."

"Amen," said Molly, raising her glass then taking a big gulp. "Like us."

Was she being sarcastic?

"So, truthfully," said Molly. "Tell me more about Reed. I never met him."

Summer set her drink on the glass-topped coffee table next to a copy of *The New Yorker* laid out like an emblem. "He's red-haired, has a great voice, a kind of southern drawl. He's from Tennessee originally and wanted to be in music until he discovered film."

"He's sort of like Magellan? 'Ah, ha! Film! I've discovered it at last'," she said in an animated Portuguese accent.

Summer looked at Molly with a frown. What went on in Molly's brain?

"I'm sorry," said Molly. "I mean, this is an odd time of life, isn't it? According to Gail Sheehy, our twenties are when we're 'forming our capacity for intimacy' without losing our tender sense of self."

"Really?"

"Grad school stuff. So why is Reed the right guy for you?"

"We can talk to each other. He respects me. We like the same vegetable, artichokes."

Molly laughed.

"He likes my poetry. He encourages me to look for my inner artist."

"Sort of like your lost inner child? Seems to me, you have plenty of that."

"What do you mean?" said Summer, sensing it was a criticism.

"You were an art history major, right?"

"Yeah. So?"

"You going to get a job in art history? With a B.A.?"

"I don't remember your being so cynical," said Summer.

"Wait until your parents and cats die," said Molly. She swirled her drink with one hand and pinched the base of her neck unconsciously with her thumb and forefinger. "You ask me," she said, "there's a reason those Muslims got up in arms over those cartoons, why the Hmong in Minneapolis get angry, and why the white supremacists shoot words back at them. Life sucks. When it comes to it: really, is anyone happy? I wouldn't be surprised if next week we hear on the news that all the life in the ocean is dying or some terrorist blew up a million people with a nuclear weapon. We've poisoned this planet, and we're killing each other."

"And so how's grad school?" said Summer with an edge.

Molly stared at her, laughed, took another sip. "Yeah, grad school's fine if you discount the committee I'm in shits with or the affair I have with one of my professors. She's a good fuck, though."

Molly was gay? Is that what she's saying? Summer felt tired of all this and grabbed her Diet Coke from the coffee table.

"I thought I'd try it," said Molly. "I mean, what good have men ever done me other than give me hope? Well...." She paused as if reviewing her internal history charts. "Initial love is always so fun, which probably explains why I had over fifty lovers as an undergrad, but I'm too much like Charlie Brown, always running for the football of love."

"You're a romantic? Hardly." Summer swirled her own drink. "I never understood why people do shitty things to themselves. And to others."

Molly grinned as if Summer had said something right. "You're quick," said Molly. "Cheryle and Tracie once told me they thought you were too clueless, but I think you have a clue. "

Summer's heart surged. "They told you this? Why would Cheryle and Tracie say such a thing?"

"Oh, they love you, don't worry. It was just conversation, one of those laughing-girls-night-out-at-Chippendales kind of things."

A cat came into the room. It had something black in its mouth. The blackness fell at Summer's feet. Summer screamed. It was a bird.

Molly merely laughed. "Hey, don't worry," said Molly, not moving. "It's not real. It's a cat toy."

"It's so real."

"For cats, it's like a blow-up sex doll."

The cat grabbed back its bird and ran quickly around Summer and out of the living room into the kitchen.

Summer stood, hand to her mouth. She'd been about to ask for Molly's phone to call Reed, but now she just wanted out.

"I'm sorry," said Summer. "I'd better get looking for an apartment."

"Oh, right," said Molly. "For you and Reed. Are you getting married?" She said it with a grin, as if it would never happen.

"I just have to leave. I'm sorry."

"Come again. Heck, soon we might be neighbors."

"Bye," said Summer like a punch, moving for the door. Once outside, she flew down the stairs.

Drops fell on her head, the first drops of a new rain. She had no raincoat or umbrella. Next to the suntan clinic stood a storefront in green, McClaren's Pub and Grill. She needed to get out of the rain. She ran and hurried in, saw it was a fairly small place. All the booths and tables were filled, but few people sat on the stools at the bar. She took a seat. Nearby, a young man held a young woman's hand. Reed never did that. Fucking Reed.

The barkeeper, a husky older woman with a wrinkled face, said, "What'll you have, Miss?"

"I'm not sure."

The lady pointed to a blackboard offering a list of beers in colored chalk. "Guinness is on tap. Today's special—along with a few whiskies."

"How about a Sea Breeze?"

"At an Irish pub? Did you look around ya?"

Summer did. This wasn't a campus crowd right now, but more older people who had had tough lives, lines on their faces that ran like trenches, and for these people, some beer in the morning hit the spot.

"A Sea Breeze," repeated the lady. "Why not? It's made with vodka and a couple juices, am I right? Cranberry and grapefruit?"

"I guess." She hadn't had a drink in forever, but she loved its name.

"I got that. Show me your ID, darlin'."

Summer did. The barkeep looked at her driver's license extra closely. "California? You visiting?"

"Moving here ahead of my boyfriend."

"Women always do the leg work, don't they?"

When the woman placed the drink before her, an older gentleman with stylish gray hair at his temples, glanced at her two stools down. His face was particularly tan and his umbrella, which he laid on the stools next to him, was wrapped up, unopened, not wet. He turned to her.

"Wow. It's really raining now!"

"You're dry."

"I'm staying out of it. Stan's the name." He held out his hand. She didn't take it.

"I have a cold," she said. "And I'm just having a quickie, and I'm gone."

"A quickie—sounds like you're my kind of gal."

She shook her head. If he thought he was witty, he wasn't.

"I'm happy to buy you the Sea Breeze," he said. "Didn't you come from upstairs above the suntan clinic? Is that the clinic, too?"

"No, an apartment."

"Yours?" He grinned.

She could only shake her head. This guy was not Mr. Subtle. Summer chugged her drink. She'd forgotten the pleasant sting of alcohol when consumed quickly. "Nice meeting you," she said and stood. Better the rain than this guy.

The barkeep came over and said, "Another, darlin'?"

"Sure, I'll buy," said Stan.

It would be so easy to get a few free drinks, manipulating this guy, and then leave, but she also knew it could be a slippery slope back to doing something stupid. No more errors. "No," she said. "Thanks anyway."

He shrugged. "I only offered because you reminded me of a painting, 'Agony in the Garden.'"

Had this guy sensed she'd been an art major? "Are you talking Bellini? The Renaissance painter?"

Stan shrugged. "I don't know. It's from the Bible. It seems like the scene was in every Catholic church in Italy."

"I don't know much about the scene," she said, strapping on her purse.

"Jesus's followers fell asleep at the garden of Gethsemane," he said, "while Jesus prayed and asked that this burden be taken from him. He could see the torches of the Roman soldiers on the way to get him. An angel came to comfort him. He was in anguish. You kind of look the same."

"Wow," she said, sitting. "All that's on my face?"

"Yeah," he said. "Another drink?"

"No. I have to get going, but... I like that you thought I was connected to a painting. Most people don't know paintings."

"I don't either. I'm just a lapsed Catholic. So what's your agony?"

She shrugged.

"How about a ginger ale?" Stan asked.

"That I'll have," she said.

Soon, she spent a half hour with Stan, blathering on about Reed, and Stan listened. "Reed didn't want to marry me when I'd asked," she told him. "He said he had his studies, but he stressed I was free to stay with him and that we could have a great life together. 'I want a good life together,' I said, 'and if you loved me, you'd move back to Minnesota with me.' Reed just thought my wish was unfair. Later, his 'maybe' had fueled me. Then he said he'd move here, and I should go back and find a place for us. That's what I'm doing here. He was even crying when he dropped me off at the airport."

"I don't think he's coming," said Stan.

"Why?"

"He's young. He's in Los Angeles. He's a selfish dreamer."

"I'd like to think he'll come, though."

"You remind me a lot of my daughter. She just entered the U, breaking up with her high school sweetheart from down in Rochester. That's where we're from. Rochester."

"The Mayo Clinic city."

"Yep, the whole city. And she wants to get into medicine."

Through the window, the rain pounded down. A couple walked by huddled together under an umbrella. They talked.

When she stood to go again, he said, "You're mighty sweet, I have to say that. And you don't have the usual Minnesota accent."

"I was born in England, actually. My father was a musician, Kyle Green."

"Of fucking Johnson, Johns, and Green? Greatest group ever on Earth. Kyle Green, really? Didn't he drive a Rolls into a hotel swimming pool?"

"A Cadillac is the rumor, never proved."

"You're like royalty. Does your boyfriend understand that?"

"He's not into music. Just film."

"I worship the ground you walk on," he said. He meant to pound the stool next to him, but instead he hit his umbrella, which flipped to the ground. "Whoops," he said. When he stood to retrieve it, she saw he was a little drunk.

Nice to meet you, Stan. Sorry," she said. "Thanks for the ginger ales."

"Con brio!" shouted Stan when she was at the door.

"Pardon?"

"It's a music term. You are full of music, 'con brio'! Stay well."

"I will. You, too. You're my angel."

She stepped out into the rain, no longer worried about getting wet. She willed herself to be wet, and cleansed, running into the downpour happily, soaring down the sidewalk, all this gray and rain and people looking at her and streets crowded and all this, and when the thunder clapped, she wasn't startled. She knew right then that Reed couldn't love her and be with her. Rather than dreading such a thought, though, she felt lighter. She felt lifted, rising into the air, sailing over stores, peaked roofs, yards, schools, churches, over the whole damn university. Hurray for the rain.

Acknowledgements

The stories in this collection were written over years and published individually at different times. Once they were put into a collection, however, the order and juxtaposition of the stories added another level, much like songs in a record album (remember those things?) In fact, thanks to editor Carol Fuchs and her observations, three of the stories' endings didn't quite work in relation to the whole. That inspired me to rewrite, even though the stories had already been published.

Over the years, eleven of my stories have appeared in *Rosebud Magazine*, five in this collection, thanks to editors Roderick Clark and John Lehman. Thank you Mr. Clark for writing the foreword to this book, making sense of the stories as a whole when I was too close to see what's here. To borrow from sportswriter Red Smith, and later Ernest Hemingway, writing is easy; just open a vein and bleed. The trick, though, is as a writer, do you publish the blood and wounds? One has to be vulnerable as a writer—and be either brave or foolish.

This isn't to say these stories are mostly autobiographical. Rather, they are true to my sensibilities—that life is like this: funny, absurd at times, sad, bittersweet, beautiful, confusing, swift, stunning, surprising, and more. I happen to teach literature and creative writing, and my favorite stories, such as those by Flannery O'Connor, Lorrie Moore, Tim O'Brien, Tobias Wolfe, and many others, share a similar sensibility.

I thank all my literate friends who read early versions of these stories, people such as Ehrich Van Lowe, Adrian Ponce, Christopher Lehmann-Haupt, Joe Cannon, Daniel Will-Harris, Sandi Milne, Preston Rose, Stewart Lindh, Danielle Davayat, Brant Kingman, Teddy Rose, Jim Chambers, Rosaleen Fitzpatrick, James Jordan, Jim Juul, Sally Shore, Nadia Pissova, Peter Seed, Karin Lowney-Seed, Judy Rudis, Brenda Friend, Mark Hughes, Jim Crawford, and others who I missed. Writing is not a solitary sport. It takes a village.

About the Author

Christopher Meeks has had stories published in several literary journals, and his books include two previous collections of stories, *Months and Seasons* and *The Middle-Aged Man and the Sea*. His latest novel, *The Chords of War,* written with Army veteran Samuel Gonzalez, Jr., takes place in the Iraq War. His novel *The Brightest Moon of the Century* made the list of three book critics' Ten Best Books of 2009. His novel *Love at Absolute Zero* also made three Best Books lists of 2011, as well as earning a *ForeWord Reviews* Book of the Year Finalist award.

His two crime novels, *Blood Drama* and *A Death in Vegas,* have earned much praise. He has had three full-length plays mounted in Los Angeles, and one, *Who Lives?* had been nominated for five Ovation Awards, Los Angeles' top theatre prize. Mr. Meeks teaches English and fiction writing at Santa Monica College, and Children's Literature at the Art Center College of Design. To read more of his books visit his website at:

www.chrismeeks.com

Made in the USA
San Bernardino, CA
05 June 2020